~THE~ SPOOK'S TALE

THE WARDSTONE CHRONICLES
by Joseph Delaney

THE SPOOK'S TALE

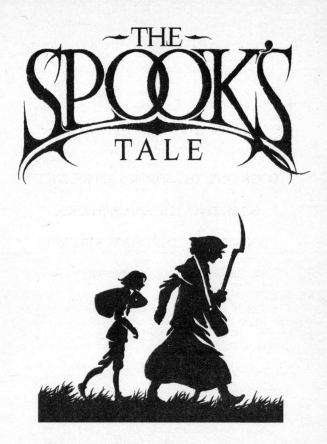

JOSEPH DELANEY

THE SPOOK'S TALE
A RED FOX BOOK 978 0 955 94460 4

Published in Great Britain by Red Fox
an imprint of Random House Children's Books
A Random House Group Company.
This first edition published specially for World Book Day 2009

1 3 5 7 9 10 8 6 4 2
Copyright © Joseph Delaney, 2009
Inside illustrations © David Frankland, 2009
Cover Illustration by Talexi

The right of Joseph Delaney to be identified as the author of this
work has been asserted in accordance with the Copyright,
Designs and Patents Act 1988.

The Random House Group Limited supports the Forest Stewardship
Council (FSC), the leading international forest certification
organization. All our titles that are printed on Greenpeace-approved
FSC-certified paper carry the FSC logo. Our paper procurement policy
can be found at www.rbooks.co.uk/environment.

Set in 8/10.5 Palatino

RANDOM HOUSE CHILDREN'S BOOKS
61–63 Uxbridge Road, London W5 5SA

www.**kids**at**random**house.co.uk
www.**rbooks**.co.uk

Addresses for companies within The Random House Group Limited
can be found at: www.randomhouse.co.uk/offices.htm

THE RANDOM HOUSE GROUP Limited Reg. No. 954009

A CIP catalogue record for this book is available
from the British Library.

Printed in the UK by CPI Bookmarque, Croydon, CR0 4TD

For Marie

This book has been specially written and published
for World Book Day 2009.
World Book Day is a worldwide celebration of books
and reading, and was marked in over
30 countries around the globe last year.
For further information please see
www.worldbookday.com
World Book Day in the UK and Ireland is made possible
by generous sponsorship from National Book Tokens,
participating publishers, authors and booksellers.
Booksellers who accept the £1 World Book Day Token
kindly agree to bear the full cost of redeeming it.

THE DEAD APPRENTICE

When I was really young, perhaps no older than six or seven, I had a terrible nightmare. It began as a pleasant dream. I was sitting on a hearth rug in the small front room of our cramped terraced house in Horshaw. I was gazing into a coal fire, watching the sparks flicker and dance before they disappeared up the chimney. My mam was also in the room. She was knitting. I could hear the rhythmical *click-click* of her needles and I felt really happy and safe. But then, over the noise of the knitting needles, I heard the dull thud of approaching footsteps. At first I thought they were outside, where my dad and brothers were working, but with a growing sense of unease I realized they were coming from the cellar.

Who could possibly be down in our cellar? The sound of the heavy boots on stone grew louder. They were climbing the steps towards the kitchen, and I knew that, whoever it was, they were coming to get me. The air suddenly developed a distinct chill – not the cold that winter brings; this was something else.

In the nightmare I tried to call out to my mam for help but I couldn't make a sound. I was mute and paralysed, frozen to the spot. The big heavy boots came nearer and nearer, but my mam just carried on sitting and knitting while my terror slowly increased. The fire flickered and died in the grate and the room grew colder and darker with each ominous approaching footstep. I was terrified – panic and dread building within me by the second.

A dark shadow shaped like a man entered the room. He crossed to where I cowered by the fire, and before I had a chance to move or cry out, he picked me up and put me under his arm. Then he took me back into the kitchen and began to descend the cellar steps, each clump of his big boots taking me deeper and deeper. I *knew* that I was having a nightmare and realized I had to wake myself up before I was taken into the absolute darkness at the foot of the cellar steps.

Struggling and straining with all my might, I somehow managed to do it just in time. I awoke, panting with fear, my brow wet with sweat, trembling at the thought of what had almost happened.

But my nightmare didn't happen just once. It came to me time and time again over the course of several years. After a while I had to tell someone so I confided in my brother Paul. I was afraid that he might laugh; that he might mock me for being so terrified of a dream. But to my surprise his eyes widened and, with a shaking voice, he revealed that he had been having *exactly* the same nightmare! At first I could scarcely believe him – but it was true! We had both been dreaming the same dream. In some ways it was a comfort, but what could this strange coincidence mean? Together we reached an important agreement.

If you were in the dream and managed to escape it, you had to wake your brother up because he might still be trapped in that nightmare, awaiting his turn to be taken down the cellar steps. Many's the night when I was sleeping peacefully, not dreaming at all, and my brother would shake me by the shoulder. I'd wake up blazing with anger, ready to thump him. But then he'd whisper in my ear, his eyes wide, his face terrified, his bottom lip trembling:

'I've just had the dream!'

I was instantly glad I hadn't thumped him – otherwise next time he might not wake me when I was having the nightmare and needed his help!

Although we told ourselves this was just a dream,

there was one thing that terrified us both. We felt absolutely sure that, if we were ever taken into the dark at the foot of the cellar steps, *we would die in our sleep and be trapped in that nightmare for ever*!

One night as I lay awake, I heard disturbing noises coming from the cellar. At first I thought I was in the dream, but slowly, with a shudder of fear, I realized these were waking sounds, not dreaming sounds. Someone was digging into the soft earth of the cellar floor with a spade. I felt that strange unnatural coldness again and heard boots climbing the stone steps, just as they did in my nightmare. Covering my ears to block out the sounds was hopeless because they didn't stop. Eventually, scared almost witless and weeping in distress, I screamed out into the darkness.

That wasn't the only time it happened, and my family's patience started to wear thin. One night, angered by the fact that I'd woken them all up again, my dad dragged me down the cellar steps, threw me into the darkness and nailed the door shut, leaving me alone and trapped there.

'Please, Dad! Please. Don't leave me here in the dark!' I pleaded.

'You'll stay there until you learn to stop waking us up!' he retorted. 'We've all got work in the morning. Think of your brothers and your poor mam. It's about time you grew up!'

'Please, Dad! Give me another chance!' I begged, but he didn't relent.

He was a good man but also hard – that's why he put me in that dark, terrifying cellar. He didn't realize what I could see and hear: things other people couldn't; things that would make the hairs on the back of your neck stand up and your heart hammer hard enough to break out of your chest. Although I didn't know it at the time, it was a consequence of what I was. I was the seventh son and my dad had been a seventh son before me. For me, the world was a very different place. I could both see and hear the dead; sometimes I could even feel them. As I sat on the cold cellar floor, I heard things approaching me in the dark, seeking me out with cold fingers and whispers, taking forms that only I could see.

I shivered with a coldness that went right through my bones and watched as a figure emerged from the darkness carrying something over his shoulder. He had big boots and looked like a miner. At first I thought it was a sack of coal he was carrying but then, to my horror, I saw that it was the limp body of a woman. I watched the tears running down the man's face as he dropped the lifeless form into the shallow pit he had dug and started to cover it with earth. As he worked, the miner gasped for air, his lungs destroyed by years of breathing in the coal dust.

It was only later that a neighbour told me the whole story. The miner mistakenly believed his wife had betrayed him by seeing another man, so he'd killed the woman he truly loved. It was a sad tale, and my pity for those who'd died so long ago slowly helped me to overcome my fear.

I didn't know it then but that was my first step towards becoming a spook. I faced my fear and slowly it ebbed away. Confronting the dark and overcoming his fear is what every spook first needs to do.

My name is John Gregory and I've worked at my trade for over sixty years. I protect the County against ghosts, ghasts, witches and boggarts. Especially witches and boggarts. If anything goes bump in the night, I deal with it.

Mine's a lonely and difficult life and I've been close to death more times than I care to remember. Now, as I approach the end of my time on earth, I'm training Tom Ward, who'll be my last apprentice.

So here's an account of my own early days. How it began for me. How I lost one vocation and gained another. How I took the first tentative step towards becoming a spook's apprentice myself.

I left home when I was twelve. Not as an apprentice to a spook – mine was a very different vocation then. I was going to travel to the seminary at Houghton and train there for the priesthood.

It was a bright crisp day in late October and I was looking forward to the long walk and eagerly anticipating the beginning of my new life.

'It's a proud day for me, son,' my poor old dad said, struggling for each breath. By then the coal dust had started to clog his lungs too, and each month they became more damaged. 'It's what every devout father wants – that one of his sons should have a vocation for the priesthood. I look forward to the day when you return to this house to give me your blessing.'

My mam wasn't there to see me leave as she'd already set off for work. As for my brothers, four of them had left home for good; of those, one was already dead: he'd been drowned while working on a canal barge that plied the route between Priestown and Caster. The two still living at home had left the house long before dawn. Andrew was an apprentice locksmith. Paul had already begun working down the mine.

Before I started out on the road to Houghton, I called in at the little parish church to speak to Father Barnes. He'd been my teacher for as long as I could remember. His inspirational sermons and tireless work to aid the poor of the parish had made me want to follow in his footsteps. Not for me days of claustrophobic darkness toiling in the mine. I was going to be a priest and help people.

As I walked down the narrow lane that led out of Horshaw, I could see someone digging in the field that belonged to the church. At first I thought it was a gravedigger, but then I noticed he was working just outside the boundary of the churchyard – not actually in holy ground. Also he seemed to be wearing a hood and gown, the garb of a priest.

However, I'd much more exciting things to think about, so I put it from my mind. I took a short cut through the hedge and began to weave my way through the gravestones towards the dilapidated church. It was always in need of repair and I could see now that there was new damage – a couple of slates missing from the roof, the result of a recent storm.

It was another of Father Barnes's routine tasks to raise the necessary funds for such repairs. When I entered the church, he was standing in the central aisle, counting copper coins into a small leather pouch.

'I've come to say goodbye, Father,' I told him, my voice echoing from the high ceiling.

'Are you looking forward to it, John?' he asked, his eyes bright with excitement. It was almost as if he were going rather than me.

'Aye, Father. I can't wait to get started on my studies. The Latin you've taught me should help me get off to a good start.'

'Well, you've been a good, diligent pupil, my boy. My hope is that one day you'll come back and take over this parish. It would be a fine thing if a member of the local flock could one day be its shepherd. That would be fitting, John. Very fitting indeed. I can't carry on for ever.'

Father Barnes was a small, wiry, grey-haired man, well into his sixties. He still looked fit and far from ready to retire, but someone would need to take over this small church one day. I remember thinking how proud that would make my dad – one of his own sons becoming the parish priest!

'It looks like last Sunday's collection plate was unusually good, Father!' I said, looking down at the pouch full of money that he was cradling in his hand.

Father Barnes smiled. 'It was a little better than usual, that's true, but what's really made a difference is the money I got from the Spook. Did you see him working by the hedge? He paid me to allow him to dig a grave there.'

Although spooks dealt with witches and got rid of ghosts and boggarts, the hierarchy of the Church considered them no better than creatures of the dark themselves: as spooks weren't ordained into the priesthood, it was thought they had no right to meddle with the dark; priests were nervous of the methods they used. Some spooks had been

15

imprisoned or even burned at the stake. However, Father Barnes was a tolerant man who took people as he found them.

'I thought he was a gravedigger,' I explained, 'but it was odd because he wasn't working in the right place.'

'Well, his apprentice died last night, and because of his trade he can't be laid to rest in the holy ground of the churchyard. But the Spook wants to bury him as close to consecrated ground as possible because it'll make the boy's family feel better. Why not, John? What harm can come of it?'

I took my leave of Father Barnes and set off north towards Houghton, my coat buttoned against the chill wind from the west. My path took me close to the place where the Spook was still digging.

The grave was almost deep enough and I could see the body of a young boy lying on the ground beside it. He looked no older than I was. The eyes of the corpse were wide open, and even from a distance it seemed to me that the dead face was twisted into an expression of absolute terror. There was something else really horrible too. Where his left hand should have been there was just a red and bloodied stump. How had he died? An accident?

I shuddered and walked on quickly but the Spook glanced in my direction. I saw that he had very bushy eyebrows and a thick head of dark hair, but the most noticeable thing about him was a very deep scar that ran the whole length of the left side of his face. I remember wondering what sort of accident had left him with such a serious disfigurement. I shuddered, wondering if a witch had done it, raking down his face with her razor-sharp talons.

The late morning and afternoon passed quickly and the sun began to sink lower in the sky. I'd no hope of reaching Houghton before nightfall and planned to spend the night in a barn or outbuilding. I'd a pack of cheese sandwiches to keep my hunger at bay so it was just a case of finding some shelter. At least it was dry, unusually for this time of year in the County, but as the sun went down, a mist began to swirl in from the west. Soon I could hardly see half a dozen paces in any direction. Somehow I wandered from the track and soon became completely lost.

It was getting colder and soon it would be totally dark. I didn't fancy the prospect of a night in the open but had little choice in the matter. I'd reached the edge of a wood and decided to settle down under a tree and try to sleep. It was then that I heard footsteps in the distance. I held my breath, hoping they would pass by, but they just came nearer and nearer. I wasn't happy at the prospect of meeting a stranger out here in the dark, miles from anywhere.

It could well be a robber, someone who'd cut my throat simply to steal the coat off my back. People sometimes went missing in the County – never to be seen again. The countryside was dangerous at night – anything could be out there.

THE WITCH'S LAIR

A figure emerged from the mist walking straight towards me. For a moment his garb made me think it was a priest, but then I realized it was a spook. He wore a hood and gown, and boots of the finest quality leather. He came up really close until I could see his scarred face. It was the same man who had been digging in the churchyard at Horshaw.

'You lost, boy?' he demanded, glaring at me from under his black bushy eyebrows.

I nodded.

'Thought so. We've been heading in the same direction for miles. You make enough noise to wake the dead! Doesn't do to draw too much attention to yourself in these parts. Where are you bound?'

'The seminary at Houghton. I'm going to study

19

there for the priesthood.'

'Are you now? Well, you won't get to Houghton tonight. Follow me – I'll see if I can find you somewhere better to bed down. This area is even more dangerous than usual, but as you're here you'd be better off in my company.'

I had mixed feelings about the offer. I felt nervous being anywhere near a spook, but at the same time it was better than spending the night on my own in the open, at the mercy of any passing robber. And what did he mean, 'more dangerous than usual'?

It was as if the Spook had read my thoughts. 'Please yourself, boy. I'm only trying to help,' he said, turning his back and beginning to walk away.

'Thanks for the offer – I'd like to travel with you,' I blurted out, something deep inside having made the decision for me.

So I followed him through the trees, glancing nervously both left and right into the mist. It was said that spirits and all manner of creepy things were towed along in the wake of a spook because of his line of work. That's why people usually crossed the road to avoid passing close to one – and here I was on a dark misty night near enough to touch him!

He finally led me to an old wooden barn and we settled ourselves down on some dry straw. There were holes in the roof and the door was missing but it wasn't raining and there was hardly any wind, so it was comfortable enough. The Spook took a lantern from his bag and lit it while I opened my pack of cheese sandwiches and offered him one.

He declined with a smile and a shake of his head. 'Thanks for the offer, boy. That's generous of you, but I'm working at present and it's my habit to fast when facing the dark!'

'Is something from the dark nearby?' I asked nervously.

He grimaced. 'That's more than likely. I buried my apprentice today. He was killed by a boggart. Do you know anything about boggarts?'

I nodded. I'd been told that boggarts were spirits; they usually made a nuisance of themselves, scaring people by breaking plates or banging on doors. But I hadn't heard of anyone being killed by one before.

'There was one that plagued the Green Bottle Tavern in Horshaw for a while,' I told him. 'It used to howl down the chimney and whistle through keyholes. It never hurt anybody though, and after a few weeks it just disappeared.'

'Sounds like a type we call a *whistler*, boy – they are mostly harmless. But there are lots of different kinds of boggart and some are more dangerous than others. For example, there are *hall-knockers*, which usually just make noises. They feed on the fear they generate – that's how they get their power. But hall-knockers sometimes change without warning into *stone-chuckers*, which can hurl large rocks and kill people. But there are even worse types of boggart. I've been trying to deal with what we call a *bone-breaker*. They rob fresh graves, digging up the corpses, then scraping off the flesh and devouring the marrow inside the bones.'

I shuddered at the gruesome picture he'd painted, but he hadn't finished yet.

'However, the worst of them develop a taste for the living. This happens when a witch gets involved. Some witches use bone-magic as the source of their dark power. What better for such a malevolent witch than to control a bone-breaker and get it to bring her what she needs!'

I shivered. 'Sounds horrible!' I told him.

'It's worse than that, boy. Soldiers fighting a battle rarely have to face such terrors. There I was, just two nights ago, on my way to bind a bone-breaker, when the boggart struck. I heard it coming across the field and I called out a warning to my apprentice. But it was too late. The boggart snatched the thumb-bone of his left hand. Well, that's what it wanted, but it took the whole hand off at the wrist. There was little I could do. I managed to stop the bleeding by binding his upper arm tightly with strips torn from his cloak. But he soon went blue round the lips and stopped breathing. The shock of the injury must have killed him.

'That was totally unexpected,' continued the Spook. 'The boggart would have had no idea we were in the vicinity. Someone must have directed it to us. I suspect a witch must have been involved . . .'

He fell silent and stared at the wall for a long time, as if reliving those terrible events. It gave me a chance to study his face. The scar was exceedingly deep and ran from high on his forehead right down to his chin. He was lucky not to have lost the sight of his left eye. The scar cut a white swathe through his eyebrow and the two separated ridges of hair were not quite in line.

The Spook glanced at me quickly. I looked away but he knew that I'd been studying his face. 'Not a pretty sight, is it, boy?' he growled. 'Another boggart did that – a stone-chucker. But that's a different story.'

'The boggart that killed your apprentice, is it close by?' I asked.

'It won't be far away, boy. It all happened less than a mile from here. Over yonder to the east,' he said, pointing through the open doorway, 'just south of Grimshaw Wood – and that's where I'll be heading at first light. The job needs finishing.'

The thought of such a dangerous boggart so close to our shelter made me really nervous and I jumped a few times when some noise outside disturbed me. But I was so tired that I eventually fell asleep.

Soon after dawn, with a brief 'Good morning' and a nod, the Spook and I parted, and I continued north through the trees. The weather had changed. It was now unseasonably warm, and dark clouds were gathering overhead. I'd travelled less than a mile when I heard the first rumble of thunder. Soon forked lightning was splitting the sky with flash after jagged flash. I'd never liked thunder – it made me nervous, and I wanted to get away from the trees and the risk of being struck by lightning.

Suddenly I saw what I took to be a ruined cottage ahead. One of the windows was boarded up, another had a broken pane and the front door hung wide on its hinges. It seemed like a good place to shelter while the storm passed. But no sooner had I stepped inside than I realized I'd made a very big mistake.

The place showed signs of very recent occupation. The ashes of a fire were still smoking in the grate of the small front room and I saw the stub of a fat candle on the window ledge; a candle made from black wax.

When I saw that, my heart began to hammer with fear. It was said that witches used such candles: they were that dark colour because blood had been stirred into the molten wax. This cottage must be a witch's lair!

I held my breath and listened very carefully. The cottage was totally silent. All I could hear was the rain drumming on the roof. Should I run for it? Was it safer out there, at the mercy of the elements? Ready to flee at the slightest hint of danger, I tiptoed to the kitchen doorway and peered through. What I saw was bad. Very bad . . .

There were bones in an untidy heap in the far corner of the flagged floor: leg-bones, arm-bones, finger-bones and even a skull. But they weren't just animal bones left over from cooking. My whole body started trembling at what I saw.

They were human bones. And amongst them were thumb-bones. Lots of them.

I turned round and made straight for the cottage door, but I was too late. I glimpsed something through the broken window. Someone was approaching through the trees – a woman dressed in black, her long gown trailing on the wet grass. The sky was very dark now and at first I couldn't make out her face. But she suddenly came to a halt and the lightning flashed almost directly overhead so I could see her clearly. How I wished I hadn't! Her expression was cruel, her eyes narrow slits, her sharp nose almost fleshless. As I watched, she tilted her head upwards and I heard her sniff loudly three times. Then she started to move more quickly towards the cottage, as if she knew I was there.

I ran back into the kitchen. Could I escape through the back door? Desperately I tried to open it. The door was locked and too sturdy to force open. There were only two places to go. Either up the stairs or down stone steps into the darkness of the cellar! It was no choice at all, so I quickly tiptoed upstairs. The witch would surely have reached the front door by now.

I crept onto the landing and saw that there were only two bedrooms. Which one should I choose? There was no time to think. I opened the door and stepped into the first one. There was no bed – just a small table and lots of rubbish on the floor: a heap of mouldering rags, pieces of a broken chair and an old pair of pointy black shoes with the soles worn right through.

I sat down on the floor and tried to keep as still as possible. I heard the witch enter the house. She crossed the front room and stepped into the kitchen. Would she come up the stairs?

Lightning flashed just outside the window, to be answered by a loud crack of thunder. The storm was now almost directly overhead. I heard the *click-click* of the witch's heels as she crossed the kitchen flags. Next the creaking of the wooden stairs. She was coming up towards me. And as she climbed, I began to feel very cold – the same sort of cold I'd experienced when my dad had locked me in the cellar and I'd come face to face with the dead miner.

Maybe the witch would go into the other room? This one was only a storeroom, but there might be a bed in the one next door. A bed where she'd settle down and go to sleep. I'd be able to sneak out of the house and make my escape then!

'Please, God! Please!' I prayed silently. 'Make her choose the other room!'

But my prayer was in vain. My last desperate hopes were dashed as the witch came directly to the room where I was hiding. For a moment she paused outside: my heart pounded in my chest, the palms of my hands began to sweat and the cold became more intense. Then she opened the door and looked down at me, her cruel eyes staring into mine so that I felt like a rabbit in thrall to a stoat. I tried to stand but found that I couldn't even move. It wasn't just fear. I was bound to the spot. Was she using dark magic against me?

To my horror, the witch pulled a knife from the pocket of her black gown. It had a long sharp blade and she held it out, moving towards me purpose-fully. Was she going to take some of my bones? She held the knife above my head and suddenly grasped me very tightly by my hair, twisting my head back-wards. She was going to kill me!

3

A SPOOK'S BONES

'Oh! I'm sorry! Really sorry!' I cried out. 'I didn't mean to come into your cottage. I didn't know it was occupied. I just wanted to shelter from the storm . . .'

'Of course you didn't *intend* to come here, child,' the witch said, her voice a cruel rasp. 'I brought you here with a *spider-spell*. I lured you into my web. And now you're in a right tangle, aren't you?'

With those words the blade swept down towards my head. I gasped in anticipation of pain and closed my eyes, but the next second she released me and I opened them again. She was holding a clump of my hair. She'd used the knife to cut it off.

'Without my help, you'll never get free – never leave this house,' she warned. 'At least not while you're still breathing. But if you're obedient, I'll let you go. So are you going to do exactly what I tell you?'

I was shaking like a leaf now and felt utterly weak and powerless. I still couldn't move – apart from my mouth, which I opened to say, 'Yes.'

'I can see you're going to be a sensible boy,' the witch continued. 'But if you get up to any tricks, I'll set *Snatcher* on you. And you wouldn't want to meet him. Snatch your bones, he will, and bring 'em straight back to me!'

By Snatcher I guessed she meant the boggart. The Spook had been right. The bone-breaker was being controlled by a witch.

'All you have to do is bring the Spook to this house,' she continued. 'He'll be hunting me down soon enough so I'll put paid to him first! You just have to bring him here!'

'Can't you just bring him here the way you brought me?' I asked.

The witch shook her head. 'Can't use the spider-spell on him – he's too old and strong and crafty. Just tell him you were going to shelter from the storm in this cottage. Then you peered through the window and saw a child here bound with rope to hooks on the wall while a witch stirred a big cauldron over a fire. That should do the trick. He'll hope to take me by surprise but I'll be ready for him!'

'What will you do then?' I asked nervously.

The witch's face cracked into a cruel smile. 'Well, a spook's bones are the most useful of all. Especially the thumbs. No doubt I'll find something useful to do with the bits of him that are left over. Nothing ever goes to waste! But let me worry about that. You just bring him here – once he's through the door, I'll do the rest and you can get on your way and forget that you ever met me. What do you say?'

It was horrible. She wanted me to lure the Spook to his death. But if I didn't do as she said, I'd never leave the witch's cottage. I'd be the one to die.

'I'll do it,' I said, feeling like a coward. But what else could I have done?

The witch gave me a wicked smile and instantly my limbs were released from the spell and I was free to move.

'Downstairs with you!' she commanded, then followed me into the kitchen and along to the small front room. She watched me from the front doorway as I walked away.

'Don't forget, child! Snatcher would love your bones! Once he sniffs this lock of hair, he'll be able to find you anywhere! No matter how far you run, he'll follow. So do as I say or it'll be the worse for you. Bring that spook here by nightfall or I'll send Snatcher after you. And you'll never see the sun rise again!'

Terrified, I set off in the direction the Spook had indicated the previous night, my mind spinning with all that had happened. I felt as if I'd stepped into a nightmare – one that I'd never wake up from.

The thunder was rumbling away into the distance and the rain was now little more than drizzle. But another storm was exploding inside my head. What if I simply turned and headed towards Houghton? Could the boggart really follow and find me any-where I went? Or was the witch just saying that to scare me? It seemed too big a chance to take. So I kept walking towards the place where the Spook should be.

What if I just told him the truth – that she'd ordered me to lure him back to the cottage? Would he be able to help me? It didn't seem likely. After all, he'd failed to protect his own apprentice against the boggart.

It didn't take me long to find the Spook. Grimshaw Wood, mainly composed of bare ash, oak and syca-more trees, lay in a narrow valley. As I approached its southern end, my feet sinking into the dank mouldering autumn leaves, I could hear someone digging in the soft earth.

There, close to the roots of an ancient oak, two men in shirt-sleeves were digging a pit. The Spook was watching them with folded arms. Close by stood a horse and cart with a large flat stone tied to the boards. As I drew nearer, the Spook turned to watch me but the men continued working, not even giving a single glance in my direction.

'What's wrong, boy? Lost again?' he demanded.

'I've found the witch,' I told him. 'I was going to shelter from the storm in what I thought was an abandoned cottage. But I looked through the window and saw a child tied up and a witch stirring a big cauldron . . .'

The Spook looked at me hard, his eyes locked upon mine. 'A child tied up, you say? That's bad. But how do you know the woman was a witch?'

I thought quickly, remembering the feeling of cold I'd experienced as she approached the cottage. 'I felt cold, really cold,' I told him. 'It's the same sort of feeling I get when I'm near a ghost – which is something from the dark like a witch, isn't it?'

The Spook nodded but looked suspicious. 'See many ghosts, do you?'

'There are two in our cellar. A miner and the wife he killed.'

'What's your name, boy?'

'John Gregory.'

The Spook looked at me thoughtfully. 'Have you any brothers, John?'

'Six,' I told him. 'I'm the last one to leave home.'

'So you're the youngest, no doubt. What about

your father? How many brothers did he have?'

'Six as well, just like me. He was the youngest too.'

'Do you know what that makes you, boy?'

I shook my head.

'It makes you a seventh son of a seventh son. You have gifts: the ability to see the dead and to deal with them if necessary; to talk to them and enable them to leave this world and go to the light. The strength to deal with witches too, and all manner of other things that serve the dark. It's a gift. Anyway, where is this cottage?' he asked, his voice suddenly very quiet.

'Back there. Not that far north of the barn where we stayed last night.'

'And you just happened to stumble upon a cottage where a witch is holding a child captive? Are you sure you're telling me the truth, boy? You're afraid, I can see that. And who can blame you if that's what you've really seen. But in my line of work it's useful to be able to tell when someone's telling a lie or holding something back. You rely on instincts and experience to do that. Looking at you, I'm getting that feeling now. Am I right, boy?'

I looked down. I couldn't meet his gaze any longer. I began to tremble. 'There is no child!' I admitted, blurting out the truth. 'The witch made me say that. She cut off a lock of my hair and said the boggart would snatch my bones if I didn't. She wants to lure you to the cottage. She said if I took you there she'd let me go. I'm sorry for lying but I'm scared. Really scared! She said I've till nightfall to bring you back to her cottage. After that she'll send her boggart after me.'

'Now we're getting somewhere,' said the Spook. 'Were you lying about feeling cold too?'

I shook my head. 'No, that's true. I was trapped upstairs and when she came into the cottage, I felt that strange chill.'

'So you really are a seventh son of a seventh son?'

I nodded.

'Well, I don't tell lies, boy, under any circumstances. So I'm going to tell you the truth, unpleasant though it may be. The witch has a lock of your hair and she can use it to weave dark spells. She could hurt you now if she wanted; make you feel seriously unwell. She can also use it to help the boggart track you down. There are mysterious lines of power under the earth – we call them ley-lines, and the County is criss-crossed with them. Boggarts use them to travel quickly from place to place. That bone-breaker could get to Houghton in the blinking of an eye and then snatch your bones just as it did with my poor apprentice. And all the priests in that big seminary wouldn't be able to help you. So you are in real danger, mark my words.

'But I'll tell you something else for nothing.

It would have done you no good at all to have got me to that cottage. She wouldn't have let you go. She'd have taken your bones too. We're both seventh sons of seventh sons and that's why our bones are so valuable to a witch. They make the dark magic she uses more powerful. Anyway, let's see what we can do to save ourselves from such a fate.'

The Spook closed his eyes, deep in thought, and said nothing for several minutes. The only sound was the spades cutting into the soft earth. I was very much aware of the passage of time. Sunset was drawing closer with every breath I took.

At last the Spook looked at me and nodded as if he'd just arrived at an important decision. 'We could go to the cottage together in full knowledge of what we face. There's a chance that I might take the witch by surprise and bind her, although there's the boggart to deal with as well. Not only that but we'd be going into the witch's territory. If she's lived in that cottage for some time, it could be full of traps and dark magic spells.

'No,' he went on, his jaw suddenly firming with decision. 'Let her come to us. Let her face what we've prepared. Sorry, lads!' he called out to the two men. 'That pit won't do now. I'm afraid we're going to have to start all over else-where . . .'

The two men rested their arms on their spades

and glared at us, their expressions a mixture of annoyance and disbelief.

'Cheer up!' called the Spook. 'I'll be paying you extra for your trouble. But we need to get a move on. Do you know Demdike Tower?'

'Aye,' the larger of the two men replied. 'Nothing but a ruin though. Place to keep well away from after dark, Mr Horrocks, that's for sure!'

'You'll be safe enough with me,' said the Spook. 'And what lingers there couldn't hurt you anyway. But we need to work fast. The boggart we're out to trap will be there soon after the sun sets, so follow me as quick as you can!'

With those words he set off at a furious pace. I followed at his heels and glanced back to see that the two men were throwing their spades onto the cart.

'Why will the boggart go to Demdike Tower?' I asked.

'You can't be that wet behind the ears! Think about it, boy. Why do *you* think it'll go there!'

Suddenly it dawned on me. 'Because I'll be there . . .'

'Aye, lad. You'll be the bait.'

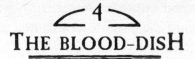

4

THE BLOOD-DISH

We reached the tower late in the afternoon. It was a crumbling abandoned ruin, part of a larger fortification that had long since been levelled by time and the elements. Only a few half-buried stones marked the boundaries of what had once been a formidable castle. Looking up at it, I remembered what the riggers had said.

'What was that about the tower?' I asked the Spook. 'You said something lingers there. Is it haunted?'

'After a fashion – but only by a ghast, which is just what's left after a spirit has gone on to the light. It's the bad part of it, the baggage the soul had to leave behind to be free of this world. It's nothing to worry about as long as you don't show fear. You see, that's what ghasts feed on, just like boggarts. It makes them more powerful. But what's a ghast when we've a malevolent witch and a bone-breaker to face? That's the least of our worries!'

To my surprise, the Spook walked past the tower and headed for the sloping wood just beyond it, where I could hear the sound of water rushing over stones.

Soon, picking our way through the trees, we were walking downstream beside a torrent of foaming water, a small river rather than a stream, the noise growing louder with every step we took. We left the bank and descended a steep rocky path to emerge on the edge of a large pool into which a wide waterfall dropped with considerable force.

The Spook pointed at the curtain of water. 'That's just about the best chance you've got, boy,' he told me. 'Creatures of the dark find it very difficult to cross running water. For example, witches can't ford a flowing stream or a river. The same applies to boggarts. Behind that waterfall there's a small recess in the rock, just big enough for you to crouch inside. You should be safe enough there, so long as the water doesn't dry up,' he said, looking up at the torrent.

'It rained hard earlier,' he continued. 'Let's just hope it rained sufficiently to fill those hills with enough to last until well after dark. On some days that waterfall is reduced to little more than a trickle. If that were to happen at the wrong moment . . .'

He didn't need to finish his sentence. I could already imagine the water ceasing to flow, the barrier upon which my life depended failing and the savage bone-breaker boggart racing towards me. The image of the apprentice without his hand flashed into my mind. I tried to shut it out but kept seeing the red stump of his wrist and the look of horror on his dead face. I also turned to look at the waterfall and whispered a silent prayer.

We walked back up to meet the riggers, who were already unloading the stone from their cart. Under the Spook's direction we carried it down through the trees. It was really heavy and it took all four of us to manage it. That done, there was a second trip to bring down the riggers' tools and other equipment, including a couple of heavy sacks. The Spook then showed them where to dig a new pit. It was close to the waterfall, under the branch of a mature rowan tree.

With only a couple of hours left to get everything prepared before dark, the riggers set to work with a vengeance and finished the pit with fifteen minutes to spare. They were sweating a lot and I suddenly realized that it wasn't just with exertion. They were nervous, but not half as afraid as I was. After all, the boggart was coming for *me*, not them.

Once the pit had been dug, the riggers went back up to their wagon, this time returning with a large barrel, which they rolled down through the trees. When opened, it proved to be half full of a disgustingly smelly, sticky mixture.

'It's just bone-glue, boy,' the Spook told me. 'Now we have to mix salt and iron into it—'

'Salt and iron?' I interrupted. 'What do you use that for?'

'Salt burns a boggart; iron bleeds away its power. The trick is to mix those two substances into this glue and coat the inside of the pit with it to keep the boggart inside – not forgetting the lid. You lure the boggart into the pit, then down comes the stone lid and it's trapped. *Artificially bound*, we call it.'

The Spook poured half a sack of iron filings into the glue and began to stir it with a big stick. While he was working, the two riggers climbed up into the tree and fastened a block and tackle to the branch. I'd seen one used at the local mill to lift heavy flour sacks. After the iron was dispersed, the Spook told me to pour the half-sack of salt in slowly while he gave the mixture another thorough stirring. That done, he used a brush to coat the inside of the pit with it.

'Can't afford to miss the tiniest bit, boy,' he told me as he worked, 'or the boggart will eventually escape!'

I looked up uneasily at the sky and the low clouds. Already the light was beginning to go. The sun couldn't be that far from the horizon by now. I hoped the Spook could see what he was doing down there in the gloom of the pit and was sealing it properly.

By now the riggers had hoisted the stone. The chain from the block had a hook at the end and this fitted through a ring in the centre of that heavy stone lid so that it was suspended directly above the pit. The Spook quickly coated the underside, then put down the brush, took something else out of his bag and polished it on his sleeve. It was a metal dish with three small holes in it close to the rim.

'This is what we call a *bait-dish*, boy. Or sometimes a *blood-dish*. And now we need the blood . . . There's no easy way to break this to you – I need some of your blood. We'll fill the dish with it then lower it down into the pit. When the boggart arrives, it'll make straight for you, hoping to get hold of your bones, but the waterfall should stop it. Denied the bones it wants, it'll sniff out your blood – which is the next best thing – then go straight down into the pit after it. While it's drinking, we'll lower the stone into position and the job's complete. So roll up your sleeve, boy. Can't say it won't hurt but it's got to be done.'

So saying, he pulled a knife from his bag and tested the blade against his thumb. The lightest of touches produced a thin line of blood.

It was sharp all right.

'Kneel down,' he commanded, 'and hold your arm over the dish.'

Very nervously I did as I was told and for the second time that day someone approached me with a knife. But whereas the witch only cut off a lock of my hair, the Spook made a cut to the inner part of my arm, just below the elbow. It hurt and I flinched, closing my eyes. When I opened them again, the blood was dripping into the dish.

'That should do,' the Spook said at last. 'Raise your arm and press the palm of your other hand hard against the cut. That'll stop the bleeding.'

I did as I was told, watching him work to distract myself from the stinging of the cut. He now produced from his bag a long chain with three smaller ones at the end, each furnished with a tiny hook. Carefully he inserted each hook into the holes in the edge of the dish, then lowered it into the pit. Once it was at the bottom, he relaxed the chain and gave a sort of flick and the hooks came free without spilling even a drop of my blood. I could see that it took skill to do that – he must have practised for a long time.

Suddenly there was a blood-curdling scream from the direction of the tower above. I shivered and locked eyes with the Spook. He nodded to signify that he'd heard it too, but the two riggers just carried on making their preparations, oblivious to the sound.

'That's the ghast I was telling you about,' the Spook explained. 'The lord who once ruled that castle on the hill had a beautiful daughter called Miriam. She was young and foolish and fell in love with a poor forester without thinking of the consequences for them both. The boy was hunted down and killed by the savage dogs her father employed to hunt deer. When she found out, Miriam threw herself from the highest window of the tower to her death on the rocks below.'

He shook his head and sighed wearily. 'Her spirit was trapped in that tower, suffering over and over again the anguish of bereavement and the fear and pain of her own death. One of my very first tasks after completing my apprenticeship was to send that poor girl's spirit to the light. Other spooks had tried and failed but I persevered and finally managed to talk some sense into her – though she left that poor tormented fragment behind. That's her ghast that you just heard cry out. As she fell, she screamed, and now the ghast relives that moment over and over again. Sometimes the sound is so strong that even ordinary folk like our two riggers hear it. That's why the ruined tower is avoided – especially after dark.

'Right, there's no time to waste!' he finished, looking at me. 'We need to get you into position before dark.

Don't worry – the recess is small but it's comfortable enough. Just don't go to sleep and fall down the waterfall!'

I didn't know whether his last remark was meant to be a joke – there was little chance of me falling asleep when a dangerous boggart was about to arrive at any moment.

The Spook led me closer to the waterfall and pointed. 'There's a narrow ledge just inside. Work your way along until you come to the recess. There are plenty of handholds, but be careful. It'll be slippery.'

I held my breath, then stepped through the curtain of water onto the stone ledge. The water was icy cold and made me gasp, but I was through it in a second. The Spook was right about the ledge being narrow; right too about it being slippery. So facing towards the rock-face and holding onto it where I could, I began to inch slowly along to my right. I shut out all thoughts of the drop behind me and muttered a few prayers to keep me calm. Moments later, to my relief, I reached the recess in the rock. It was big enough to sit in, and when I drew my knees up to my chest, my boots were just clear of the falling water. It was cold and damp and I hoped I wouldn't have to spend the whole night there. But anything was better than being at the mercy of the boggart.

* * *

I didn't have to wait long. It grew darker and darker, and by the end of twenty minutes it was difficult to see my hand in front of my face. Sounds became significant then. Someone coughed in the distance from the direction of the pit. Moments later I heard the screech of an owl followed almost immediately by the scream of the ghast. The most important noise of all was the comforting one of that screen of water falling into the pool below. But it wasn't long before I began to worry. Was the noise lessening? If so, how long before it became just a trickle and gave no protection at all?

Then I heard a faint scream in the distance. At first I thought it was the ghast again but it grew steadily louder; added to this was what sounded like a ferocious wind gathering speed – one so powerful that it could strip the summer leaves off trees or rasp the flesh from living bones. And then the sound took on another dimension, as if a third note had been added to harmonize with the other two. This was the sort of rumbling growl that a very big and dangerous animal might make as it rushed towards its prey . . . rushed towards *me*! I realized then that this was the boggart.

Louder and louder grew the three sounds; nearer and nearer came the boggart – until suddenly it was right in front of the waterfall, the noise so loud that I wanted to put my hands over my ears. But I didn't. I kept perfectly still, too scared to even twitch an eyebrow. All I could see was a sort of red glow shining through the water, but I knew the terrible creature was there, threatening me: it sounded now as if huge teeth were being gnashed and ground together hardly more than an arm's length away. But for that protective curtain of water it would already have snatched my bones. I would be dead like the Spook's poor apprentice.

I don't know how long it waited there. The glow kept brightening and fading and moving from side to side as if it were searching for a gap in the curtain of water. This was the scariest moment of all: I remembered the Spook had told me that the inside of the pit had to be coated thoroughly because a boggart could escape through the narrowest of openings. Would it find one in the waterfall? I wondered, my heart pounding in my chest.

Its search lasted just a few minutes – though it seemed a lot longer. Then, to my relief, it was gone. Still I sat rigid, not daring to move until at last I heard the sudden whirr of chains. The boggart must be in the pit, attracted by my blood in the bait-dish, and the riggers were lowering the stone to trap it inside.

Finally I heard a thud and guessed that it must be the stone dropping onto the rim of the pit, hitting the soft earth. Then, at last, the Spook called out to me:

'Right, boy, the boggart's safe and sound. Out you come!'

Weak with relief, I did as I was told, moving carefully back along the slippery ledge and ducking out through the cold waterfall again. The Spook had lit a lantern and was sitting beside it on the stone lid of the boggart pit, which was now safely in position. The boggart was bound. My nightmare was over at last.

'It all went according to plan,' said the Spook. 'Did you hear the boggart?'

'Aye, I heard it approach. I could see it too, glowing red through the waterfall.'

'That it did, boy. You're a seventh son of a seventh son all right. It was red because it had fed earlier in the day – they take blood if they can't get their favourite bones. But when it attacked, those two riggers wouldn't have seen or heard a thing. Good job too, or they'd have run a mile and we'd never have got the stone into place. I think they heard it slurping your blood down in the pit though. One of them started to moan with fear and the other's hands were shaking so much he could hardly manipulate the chain! Well, sit yourself down, boy. It's not over yet . . .'

I sat down next to him on the stone. What did he mean, it wasn't over yet? I wondered. But I said nothing for a while. The riggers were still busy taking the block and tackle down from the rowan branch and collecting their tools together.

'We'll be off now, Mr Horrocks,' the taller one said, holding up a lantern and touching the rim of his cap in respect.

'You did a good job, lads, so get you gone,' said the Spook. 'There's a witch heading this way from the north-west, so I'd take any direction but that.'

With those words he counted money into the man's palm in payment for the work done, and both riggers set off up the slope as if the devil himself were chasing them. When they'd gone, the Spook patted me on the shoulder. 'You've been brave and sensible so far, boy. So I'm going to be honest with you again and tell you what's likely to happen. To start with, there's no way you can go to Houghton until all this is finally sorted out. You see, that witch still has that lock of your hair . . .'

With all the danger and excitement I'd forgotten all about the witch. Suddenly I began to feel scared again. I'd disobeyed her, and telling the Spook the truth had led to her boggart being trapped in the pit. She'd want vengeance for that.

'Using it,' the Spook continued, 'she can do you serious mischief so we have to get it back and destroy it – otherwise you'll never be safe. And for now the best place you can be is by my side. Understand?'

I nodded nervously and peered out into the darkness

beyond the circle of light cast by the lantern. 'Will she come here?' I asked.

'That's what I believe, boy, but hopefully not before dawn. She'll be easier to deal with in daylight. You see, she'll come to find out what's happened to the boggart. Once she sees it's bound, the witch will try to free it. That will give me a chance to sort her out once and for all. I'll bind her with my silver chain and carry her back to my garden at Chipenden. She'll spend the rest of her life bound in a pit and the County will be a much safer place!'

He made it sound easy, but we spent a long and uncomfortable night waiting for the witch. I didn't sleep at all and neither did the Spook. Dawn came and the morning drew on. Once it was past noon and into early afternoon, the Spook began to pace up and down, looking increasingly concerned.

Finally he turned to face me. 'Looks like I was wrong, boy. We're dealing with a particularly crafty witch. She must have worked out that I've bound her boggart and that I'm planning to trap her. So she won't come here. No, I'm afraid we're going to have to seek her out.'

'But won't that mean going into her cottage? You said there'd be lots of dark magic traps and snares there!'

'That's true enough, boy. But what choice do we

have? We might as well get it over with – follow me!'

With those words he picked up his bag and staff and set off north-west at a rapid pace while I struggled to keep up. At first we walked in silence but as we drew nearer to the witch's cottage, the Spook slowed down and dropped back to walk beside me.

'We're not going to get there much before dark, boy, so we'll have to wait until morning to deal with her. It'll be easier and safer then. But I'm going to explain what we're up against so that you know the worst . . .

'The land around her cottage will no doubt be full of danger, with dark magic spells and snares ready to trap us. But inside her dwelling – well, that doesn't bear thinking about. I expect the witch will be waiting down in the cellar. That's what witches often do when at bay. They find an underground lair, a place of darkness, and defend it with every dirty trick that a lifetime of malevolence has taught them. This isn't going to be easy, boy.'

As we approached the cottage through the trees, it was already getting dark. We were moving slowly and cautiously in case she'd set any snares. There was a sudden rustle from above and I shuddered with fear as I saw a pair of large eyes staring down at us from a branch. It was an owl, and it suddenly took off, gliding away almost soundlessly through the trees towards the cottage.

'If I'm not mistaken, that was the witch's familiar,' said the Spook. 'There was an owl about last night when you were safely positioned behind the waterfall – almost certainly the same one – so it must have been watching what we were doing then.

'A familiar can be something as small as a toad or as large as a big dog. Whatever it is, it'll be the eyes and ears of the witch. You see, a witch usually uses what we call *long-sniffing* to see what's about to happen – especially if danger threatens. But I'm not worried about that – long-sniffing doesn't work on seventh sons of seventh sons. So she has to find another way. Bone-magic is stronger than blood-magic, but more powerful than both put together is familiar-magic. And a witch strong enough to control a boggart may also have a familiar doing her bidding. Most likely it's that owl. If so, the witch will already know what's happened to her boggart. Just as she'll know now that we're very close to her cottage.'

We settled down in the trees just within sight of the cottage, ready for a long vigil. The Spook had told me that we had to stay alert and couldn't afford to sleep even for a moment. We'd only been there about ten minutes or so when I started to feel unwell. It was as if someone very strong had me in a bear hug and was squeezing my chest. I couldn't get my breath and started to gasp and choke.

The Spook turned towards me. 'You all right, boy?' he asked.

'I'm finding it hard to breathe,' I told him.

'Have you ever had problems like this before?' he asked.

I shook my head. It was getting difficult to speak. But after a few moments the pain went away and I could breathe more easily. My brow was wet with sweat but I was relieved. It felt so good just to be able to fill my lungs and not fight for air. But my relief was short-lived. Within minutes the pain came back worse than ever. This time the constriction of my chest was so tight that I couldn't breathe at all. I lurched to my feet in panic, the world spun about me and I felt myself falling into darkness.

5
THE SILVER CHAIN

The next thing I knew I was lying on my back looking up at the moon through the bare branches of a tree.

The Spook helped me to sit up. 'It's the witch,' he told me. 'She's using that lock of your hair to do you serious harm. I thought you were a goner then. You see, she's trying to force my hand. She wants me to face her now while it's still dark and her powers are in the ascendancy. So I don't have any choice – the next time she might kill you. You'll have to come with me: it's far too dangerous to leave you out here alone. Your best chance is still to stick close to me . . .'

He helped me to my feet. I felt weak but stumbled after him as he made directly for the cottage. We hadn't taken more than a dozen paces when I began to feel unwell again. But this time it was different. Rather than feeling breathless, my body was now so heavy and weary I could hardly take another step.

Then I began to see things beneath the trees – objects that shone white in the moonlight. Beads of sweat formed on my forehead and ran into my eyes. I was about to call out to the Spook when he came to a sudden halt and motioned with his staff that I should stop too. When he turned slowly back to face me, the moonlight illuminating his face, I could see sweat on his brow too.

'How are you, boy? You don't look well to me. Not well at all . . .'

'Is it the witch again?' I asked. 'I feel really sluggish and heavy.'

'Yes, she's the one who's making you feel like that – that's certain. She's not using your lock of hair though, because I can feel it too. See those bones over there?' he asked, pointing with his staff.

He indicated one of the white things I'd noticed. Now I could see that it was actually a heap of small bones – those of a rabbit, long since dead. I glanced about and saw other similar mounds. Some were the bones of birds; a particularly large pile in the distance looked like the remains of a deer.

'We're right on the edge of a dark magic snare,'

said the Spook. 'It's what we call a *bone-yard*. Anything that enters the snare's in trouble right away. Your bones start to get heavy; after a while you can't move at all and die a slow death of starvation – that's if you've not gone too far in. Later the witch comes to collect the bones she needs for her spells. She can make do with animals but she's really waiting for a person to blunder into her yard. Right near the centre, victims suffer a speedier death. Their bones become so heavy they're crushed to powder. Now, we need to start walking backwards, boy. Do it nice and slowly and take deep breaths – otherwise you might faint and there's no way I'd be able to carry you out of this trap.'

I did as he instructed, breathing evenly and deeply and taking slow backward steps. It was hard and I began to sweat with the exertion. At one point I almost lost my balance and just managed to recover in time. Falling would be as bad as fainting. Gradually the heaviness of my body eased, and eventually I felt quite comfortable in my skin again.

'Now follow me. We need to skirt this trap and go the long way round,' the Spook told me.

As we took a roundabout route towards the witch's lair, a thought struck me. 'I was lucky not to blunder into that snare yesterday when I first saw the cottage,' I commented.

'Luck wasn't involved, boy. That spider-spell

the witch spun to lure you to her door would have guaranteed that you got there safely; it tugged you along by the safest path. Anyway, now we come to the dangerous part. I've got to go in and find where she's hiding . . .'

We were at the edge of the trees and could now see the front of the cottage. Getting inside would be easy. The door was hanging open as if inviting us to enter, but it was utterly dark within. The Spook led us forward but paused at the threshold. He placed his staff on the ground and took the lantern from his bag, quickly lighting it. Next he pulled out his silver chain and coiled it around his left wrist before passing the bag to me.

'You'll have to carry that for now, boy. Bring my staff too and hand it to me quickly if I need it.'

'How will I know when to give it to you?'

He gave me a withering look, then smiled grimly. 'Because I'll shout for it so loud it'll blow your socks off! Look, just stay alert. As we search the cottage, stay five steps behind me. I need room to work. I'm going to try and bind the witch with my chain. That's our best hope of dealing with her quickly.'

So saying, he turned, picked up the lantern with his right hand and led the way into the witch's cottage. I followed close behind carrying his heavy bag and staff, my knees starting to tremble. The lantern was casting strange shadows on the walls and ceiling and I started to feel very cold. The unnatural cold that warns that something from the dark is very near.

The Spook advanced slowly and cautiously through the small front room and into the kitchen. The witch could be anywhere and might attack at any moment. He glanced at the heap of bones in the corner and shook his head; then, sighing deeply, he began to climb the stairs. I followed at a distance, my legs trembling with every step. My back was now to the kitchen and I didn't know if I was more afraid of what might lie in wait ahead of us or what might lurch out of the darkness behind. I could almost feel the witch's talons clawing at my ankles as I climbed. I glanced nervously over my shoulder but the kitchen was empty. We checked each bedroom in turn. Again, nothing. We would have to go down to the cellar. The prospect of that scared me more than anything. I hated cellars. It brought back memories of my recurring nightmare. That and the time my dad had thrown me into the cellar at home and nailed the door shut.

We went down to the kitchen again and the Spook strode purposefully towards the cellar steps. I let him go down five before I began my own slow descent. There was a bend in the stair; beyond it, the steps continued down at right angles. When he reached that bend, the Spook held the lantern high. I was facing his left-hand side, and from the expression on his face and the way his whole body suddenly straightened, I knew that he could see the witch waiting below.

I was right! He uncoiled the silver chain with one flick of his wrist and prepared to cast it downwards. But no sooner had he done so than the ground seemed to move beneath my feet. That was impossible. How could solid stone steps do that? But whatever I felt, further down the effect must have been much stronger. Before he could cast the chain the Spook tottered, lost his balance, then fell headlong and was lost to view.

Instantly I was plunged into darkness. The Spook, chain and lantern were down in the cellar. He was at the mercy of the witch. My heart hammering, I turned to flee. I could do nothing against a witch. How could I help him? I had to get away or she'd take my bones too.

But then something stopped me. What it was or why I changed my mind, I can't explain to this day. Maybe it was self-preservation – because if I abandoned the Spook, the witch would still have a lock of my hair. Later, she could release the boggart and send it after me. Or perhaps it was something inside me – the courage that a spook needs in order to face the dark and do his dangerous job.

Whatever it was, I edged cautiously down

the steps and, hardly able to believe what I was doing, my heart pounding in my chest, peered round the corner. Rather than looking down into absolute darkness, I could see almost everything in the cellar. The lantern was lying on its side but hadn't gone out. The Spook was on all fours, head hanging, forehead almost touching the floor. The witch was crouching over him with a knife in her hand. In just moments she'd take his life. But so intent was she upon her evil business that she didn't look up and see me on the steps. No doubt she'd expected me to be long gone.

The Spook looked up at the witch and gave a groan of fear. 'No! No! Not like this!' he pleaded. 'Please, God, don't let it end like this!'

Without thinking, I put down the bag, lifted the Spook's staff and ran down the steps, straight towards the witch. At the very last moment she looked up at me, but she was too late. I swung the staff and hit her hard on the forehead. She fell backwards with a cry, the knife flying out of her hand, though she was up on her knees again almost at once, face twisted with fury. And for the second time I felt the solid ground move beneath my feet, this time with a violent lurch that brought me down hard onto the cellar floor, jolting the staff from my grasp.

I was flat on my back and started to sit up, but within seconds the witch was on me, both hands around my throat, trying to choke the life from me. Her face was close to my own, her eyes wild, her open mouth showing sharp teeth. Her foul breath made me heave. It stank like a cat's or a dog's – of stale meat with a sweet hint of blood.

I glanced to my right and saw the Spook struggle shakily to his feet and stagger against the cellar wall. He was in no fit state to help me. If I didn't do something, I'd be dead in moments!

I gripped the witch by the shoulders and tried to throw her off me but she was squeezing my throat so hard I couldn't breathe. I could feel myself weakening, my sight darkening, and I desperately reached out with both hands, trying to find the Spook's staff. It wasn't there. But then my left hand closed over something else. The silver chain!

I gripped it and swung it across. It caught her head a glancing blow and she screamed, withdrew her hands from my throat, and pressed them to her face. I whipped the chain back in the opposite direction, this time catching her on the chin. She stood up, then staggered and dropped to her knees. I felt a hand on my shoulder and looked up to see the Spook standing over me, breathing hard.

'Here, boy. You've done well. Now give me the chain.'

I handed it to him, and after quickly coiling it about his wrist, he sent it soaring aloft with a crack and it dropped over the witch and coiled about her tightly. She rolled over and over, her eyes bulging from their sockets, the chain tight against her teeth and binding her arms to her side.

'She's bound good and proper now,' the Spook said, smiling grimly. 'I owe you a big thanks, boy.'

With the witch safely bound, we searched the cottage and the Spook made a fire outside and burned the things he found: powders, herbs and a book of dark magic which he called a grimoire. Eventually he found my lock of hair in a leather pouch which the witch wore on a chain around her neck. He burned that too – at last I was safe and began to feel a lot better.

We sat by the fire for a while, both of us locked into our own thoughts, until a question came into my mind and I broke the silence.

'What was it on the steps that made you fall?' I asked. 'I felt the ground tremble beneath my feet. Later, in the cellar, it gave another lurch and I fell too.'

'One of the snares she'd set to defend herself, boy,' the Spook said, throwing another handful of the witch's possessions into the flickering flames of the bonfire. 'It's called *Slither*, a spell that causes the victim to feel unsteady on his feet, lose his balance, slide and fall. It nearly did for me all right.

Even if you anticipate it, little can be done. As I said, I owe you a big thanks and I'd like to make you an offer. How would you like to train as a spook? As it happens, I'm looking for an apprentice to replace the one I've just lost. Would you be interested? I need a brave lad for my line of work.'

'Thanks for the offer but I'm going to be a priest,' I told him. 'It's something I've wanted to do for a long time.'

'It's your choice, boy. I won't say anything against the priesthood because some of them are good men who mean well—'

'Father Barnes works hard to help the poor,' I interrupted. 'He's spent his whole life helping people. I want to be like him.'

'Well, good luck to you then, young John. But if you ever change your mind, you can find my house near Chipenden village, west of the Long Ridge. Just ask any of the locals. My name's Henry Horrocks. They'll point you in the right direction.'

With that we parted. Carrying the witch over his shoulder, the Spook set off towards Chipenden, where he'd bind her in a pit. I watched him walk away and supposed that would be the last I'd ever see of him.

I continued my journey to Houghton and began to train for the priesthood. I did become a priest, but not for long though that's another story. But as a young man of twenty, I eventually went to Chipenden and asked Henry Horrocks if he would train me as a spook.

He took a while to make up his mind. Could you blame him? After all, it had taken me a long time to change mine! I was far older than the boys he usually trained. But he remembered what I'd done back in that dark cottage when we'd faced the dangerous witch.That finally decided him.

I became his apprentice. His last one. Finally, after his death, I inherited his house at Chipenden and began working as a spook from there. Now, after all these years, I'm training Tom Ward. He'll be *my* last apprentice. The house will belong to him and he'll be the new Spook. Our work will go on. Someone has to fight the dark.

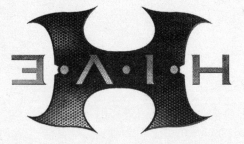

interception point

MARK WALDEN

BLOOMSBURY

LONDON BERLIN NEW YORK

Also by Mark Walden

H.I.V.E. Higher Institute of Villainous Education
H.I.V.E. The Overlord Protocol
H.I.V.E. Escape Velocity

Bloomsbury Publishing, London, Berlin and New York

First published in Great Britain in 2009 by Bloomsbury Publishing Plc
36 Soho Square, London, W1D 3QY

A CIP catalogue record of this book is available from the British Library

ISBN 978 0 9559 4460 4

All papers used by Bloomsbury Publishing are natural, recyclable
products made from wood grown in well-managed forests.
The manufacturing processes conform to the environmental
regulations of the country of origin.

Typeset by Dorchester Typesetting Group Ltd
Printed in the UK by CPI Bookmarque, Croydon, CR0 4TD

1 3 5 7 9 10 8 6 4 2

www.bloomsbury.com
www.bloomsbury.com/hive

chapter one

Otto fired the grappler line into the darkness overhead, the mono-filament cable reeling silently into the unit mounted on his wrist as he rose up into the shadows. He closed his eyes, listening carefully. He doubted that his target would make any sound to give away their location, they were too good for that. Otto was acutely aware that he was as much the hunted as the hunter here – not a feeling he liked. He flipped the switch on the side of the mask he was wearing and activated the visor's night-vision mode. The dark cavern around him was bathed in a green glow but there was still no sign of his target.

Otto took a deep breath and felt a now familiar sensation as his mind connected with the world of invisible electronic data that surrounded him. Since his confrontation with Number One a few months ago he had found it easier and easier to channel his unique abilities and he hoped that now they might give him the extra edge he needed. He could feel the surveillance devices that were mounted in the walls of the cavern, their streams of transmitted data flowing outwards, but there was something else there too, almost too faint to sense – the simple circuitry of a night-vision system identical to his own, somewhere nearby. Somewhere very nearby . . . somewhere directly behind him!

Otto suddenly felt something hard press against the back of his head.

'Bang! You're dead,' a familiar voice whispered in his ear.

Without thinking Otto connected instantly with the rudimentary systems of his target's own grappler unit and triggered the release mechanism. There was a yelp from behind him and the pressure vanished from the back of his head. He glanced downwards at the flailing figure tumbling away beneath him and splashing into the cold, dark water below.

'Lights!' a voice barked from the darkness and the cavern was lit up by numerous bright white arc lights mounted in the walls. Otto closed his eyes against the glare, his night-vision system overwhelmed by the sudden flare of illumination.

'Get down here, Malpense!' Raven shouted.

Otto fired the grappler on his other wrist and swung easily down on to the steel platform mounted along one wall of the grappler training cavern, landing softly just a couple of metres from Raven. The look on her face was enough to chill the blood: she was not pleased and when she was not pleased people had a nasty habit of dying.

'What have I told you about letting your target get the drop on you like that?' Raven said, her Russian accent becoming more pronounced, as it often did when she was angry.

'Oh, she got the drop on me all right,' Otto replied with a sly smile. 'Quite a long drop actually.'

Shelby Trinity pulled herself up on to the platform, still dripping wet, and threw her black mask to the floor.

'Malpense, you no good, slimy, cheating rat!' she shouted, striding towards him.

'Hey!' Otto said with a grin, holding his hands up in front of him. 'I'm not the one who accidentally triggered

their grappler release.'

'I did no such thing,' Shelby said angrily, 'and you know it.' She jabbed a finger into his chest. 'You used your creepy computer mojo, I had you cold.'

'Would I do that to you?' Otto asked innocently.

'Enough!' Raven snapped. 'You both failed as far as I'm concerned. Otto, you let Shelby get too close, you rely too much on your special abilities and not enough on your other senses. One day that will end up costing you dearly. Shelby, you should have taken the shot when you had it instead of giving up the element of surprise just to say something clever. Typical American. Too many movies.'

'But I . . .' Shelby replied.

'No,' Raven said quickly. 'I do not want to hear excuses. Otto, you will get the victory credit for this exercise but neither of you should feel pleased with your performance today. If this were a real operation you'd both be dead.'

Otto and Shelby nodded. They knew better than to argue with Raven. She may have been one of their tutors at H.I.V.E. but she was also one of the world's deadliest assassins and not someone that you talked back to, regardless of what they had been through with her in the past few months.

'Go and get changed, you have a Logistics and Operations lesson to get to.' Raven watched the pair of them leave. They were both excellent pupils, perfect Alpha-stream material, the leaders of the future, but they had a lot to learn.

☻☻☻

Maximilian Nero sat at his desk reading the latest report on the reconstruction of H.I.V.E.'s hangar bay. The Higher Institute of Villainous Education was a unique facility, the

world's first and only school of applied villainy. Hidden within the hollowed-out interior of a volcanic island, its location was still one of the world's most closely guarded secrets. H.I.V.E. had been training the nefarious operatives of G.L.O.V.E., the Global League of Villainous Enterprises, for many years, and as its headmaster, Dr Nero had dealt with many perilous situations. Few had been so desperate though as the recent events at the school that had left the hangar bay destroyed and had very nearly resulted in the death of every single person on the island.

A message popped up on the display mounted on Nero's desk, interrupting his thoughts. He touched the screen to accept the incoming call. The screen lit up, displaying the face of Diabolus Darkdoom, the recently appointed new head of G.L.O.V.E.

'Good morning, Diabolus, what can I do for you?' Nero asked, sensing immediately that something was wrong.

'A situation has arisen that requires our immediate attention,' Darkdoom said calmly.

'What can we do to help?' Nero asked.

'An operation in Paris has gone badly wrong. One of our operatives was captured during what we thought would be a straightforward surveillance mission. This by itself would not be a problem but there has been a . . . complication.'

'Go on,' Nero replied.

'The operative in question was wearing a thermoptic camouflage suit, a suit that did not function as required when he was captured.'

Nero immediately understood the true nature of the problem. The thermoptic camouflage suit was the jewel in the technological crown of G.L.O.V.E. It enabled the wearer to appear invisible for short periods of time,

4

projecting a perfect holographic image of the user's surroundings and masking their infrared heat signature. It was a system that gave G.L.O.V.E. operatives a huge advantage. As such all of the suits used in the field were fitted with a self-destruct device that should detonate as soon as the suit was removed by force. The device could even be remotely activated while the operative in question was still wearing it, though most operatives were unaware of that fact for obvious reasons.

'So I take it the suit has fallen into the wrong hands,' Nero said coolly.

'Indeed,' Darkdoom replied. 'The worst hands imaginable in fact.'

'H.O.P.E.,' Nero said quietly. The Hostile Operative Prosecution Executive had become an even greater thorn in G.L.O.V.E.'s side since the recent near-disastrous events. In addition to almost destroying H.I.V.E., they had captured Nero himself and very nearly succeeded in assisting Number One, G.L.O.V.E.'s previous leader, with his insane plan to take over the world. Unfortunately the world's security forces still regarded H.O.P.E. as one of their most vital assets, blissfully unaware of its involvement in that nightmarish plot.

'So I'm sure you can understand the need for a swift and decisive response here,' Darkdoom said, 'a response that will require the intervention of one of your most *gifted* students. Someone, in particular, who would be able to penetrate an automated security system that they have never seen before with almost no preparation or even any idea of what the said security system was capable of.'

'Malpense,' Nero said, with a frown. Otto Malpense had done more than anyone else to thwart Number One's plan and Nero had promised himself that he would try to

keep the boy out of harm's way for a while.

'You know that I wouldn't ask this if I thought that there was any other way but my experts have analysed the situation and can come up with no alternative retrieval operation that would have any chance of success in the time available.'

'I have my own experts,' Nero replied. 'Perhaps they can find a solution?'

'I am sure that Raven will have some ideas that could work but the suit is already being prepared for transport. We have twelve hours before it is in the hands of H.O.P.E.'s scientists at their facility in the Alps. I would love to be proved wrong, but my own experts advise me that this is our only chance.'

'Send me a brief,' Nero said with a sigh. 'I'll see what we can do.'

☺☺☺

Laura and Wing sat outside the grappler training cavern waiting for their friends to emerge.

'I hope they have not hurt each other too badly,' Wing said with a slight smile.

'Oh, I'm sure Shelby won't have been too rough with him,' Laura chuckled.

'Let us hope so,' Wing replied. 'No doubt Raven will have made sure that it did not get too far out of hand.'

'You never know with those two – things have got a little too . . . competitive recently,' Laura sighed.

The grappler session had been one of the semi-regular series of tests that H.I.V.E. constantly subjected its pupils to and Otto and Shelby had become rather obsessed with seeing which one of them would achieve the best results at the end of the programme. So far their scores had been

pretty much even but as the series of exercises had drawn towards a close the battle to be the Alpha-stream top dog had become rather personal. The difference in their scores was so small now that it had all come down to this final trial and Laura was secretly glad that the matter would be decided one way or the other today. If she had to listen to one more argument about who was going to win, she'd probably go mad.

Suddenly the steel doors sealing the entrance of the training cavern rolled aside and Otto and Shelby walked out. Shelby had a face like thunder and Otto was looking just a little bit too pleased with himself.

'Brace yourself,' Wing said with a sigh.

'So . . . um . . . how'd it go?' Laura asked as cheerfully as possible.

'I thought it went quite well,' Otto said casually, 'but Shelby seems to have mistaken the whole thing for a swimming lesson.'

'Rat boy here obviously realised that I was too good for him,' Shelby snarled, jerking a thumb at Otto. 'He had to cheat to win, like that's a surprise to anybody.'

'Cheat? *Moi?*' Otto said with a look of mock innocence. 'I can't help it if you don't know how to handle the equipment properly.'

'Guys –' Laura tried to interrupt.

'Well, you'd better check all your equipment real carefully in the future,' Shelby snapped. 'You never know when someone might sabotage your rig, do you?'

'Nothing worse than a sore loser,' Otto said happily and walked off down the corridor towards their next lesson with Shelby right behind him.

'I'm not the loser here, computer brain.'

Laura and Wing watched them walking away.

'Well, it looks like that went well,' Laura sighed, rolling her eyes.

'Would it be against school rules for me to render them both unconscious?' Wing asked.

'At this point, I don't really care,' Laura said, shaking her head, and hurried down the corridor after her bickering friends.

☢☢☢

'Is there an alternative?' Nero asked.

'Against a target like this, I fear not,' Raven said, turning off the monitor that she and Nero had been studying for the past half-hour.

'And you're sure they're ready for this?' Nero asked, sounding worried.

'No, Max, there are too many unknowns involved here, but the same was true in London and we pulled that off.'

Nero thought back to the events of a few months earlier when Raven and the students in question had managed to access the Deepcore database, buried far below MI6 headquarters. It had been an audacious and daring mission and if it had not been successful he might very well still be languishing in a H.O.P.E. detention cell.

'Do they all have to go?' Nero asked.

'I have honestly never worked with a better infiltration team. But they must learn to function better as a unit,' Raven replied. 'Let me brief them and see how they respond.'

'Very well,' Nero said, 'but, Natalya, make it quick. Time is not on our side.'

Raven nodded and walked out of the room. Nero watched her go, unable to shake the sense that there was something very wrong with the whole situation.

chapter two

'So you can see that the construction of a secret facility is a complicated and time-consuming process. Not only does one have to choose a suitably discreet and remote location, one must also use a workforce that is either entirely trustworthy or entirely disposable. The choice is yours.'

Otto found the Logistics and Operations lessons fascinating. Ever since his arrival at the school he had wondered how one would go about constructing a hidden base like H.I.V.E. Mr Rictor, their tutor, may not have been the most enthralling speaker but the information he was sharing was fascinating.

'Even more complicated, perhaps, is the means by which one defends such a facility. For example, the inclusion of a self-destruct mechanism is a practical necessity but experience has shown that this can prove to be a vulnerability . . .'

Mr Rictor suddenly stopped as the door to the classroom hissed open and Raven walked into the room. There was a brief whispered conversation between the two of them and then he glanced up the tiered rows of seats in the room, looking straight at Otto and his friends.

'Students Malpense, Fanchu, Brand and Trinity, will you please accompany Raven,' Mr Rictor said impassively.

Otto and the others exchanged brief curious looks before packing up their notes as all around them whispered conversations started. Otto and the others had

achieved a certain amount of notoriety amongst the students of H.I.V.E. and was sure to set the wheels of the school's rumour mill grinding. The four of them walked down the stairs and followed Raven out of the room.

'Trouble?' Wing whispered to Otto.

'I think that's a safe bet,' Otto said softly.

They walked in silence for a couple of minutes until Raven stopped and opened the door to one of the school's briefing rooms, ushering them inside.

'Please, be seated,' Raven said, gesturing to the seats that surrounded the large table in the centre of the room. 'There is an urgent situation with which we require your assistance. A thermoptic camouflage suit has been captured by H.O.P.E. and is at this very moment being prepped for transport to the facility that you are all familiar with in the Alps. G.L.O.V.E. has tasked us with the retrieval of this item before it can be reverse-engineered by H.O.P.E.'s scientists, something that we simply cannot allow to happen. Normally such a retrieval operation would be carried out by senior G.L.O.V.E. operatives but in this case there are some unique challenges that it is felt only the four of you would be able to overcome. The suit is being transferred to H.O.P.E. headquarters in this . . .'

Raven punched a button on the control panel in front of her and a holographic projection sprang upwards from the centre of the table. There, hovering in mid-air, slowly rotating, was a three-dimensional model of a sleek, heavily armoured train.

'This computer model has been constructed from surveillance footage stolen by our source within H.O.P.E. We know little more than the external appearance of the train and the fact that it is entirely automated and has no crew. We have approximately ten hours before it is due to arrive

at H.O.P.E.'s headquarters, which means we must strike swiftly and decisively. Otto, your abilities will be essential for us to accurately assess this train's defences and capabilities, but I want all four of you on this mission. Your combined skills should mean that you will be able to deal with whatever defensive systems it is equipped with. If the thermoptic camouflage suit falls into our enemy's hands we lose one of our most critical technological advantages, and I for one do not want to be constantly worrying that every shadow might be an invisible H.O.P.E. operative.'

Raven paused and looked around the table. From any other group of students she might have expected to see panic or confusion but the four faces that stared back at her just seemed calm and determined.

'Questions?' Raven asked.

'Do we have the route?' Otto asked.

'Yes,' Raven replied, hitting another button on the control panel. A three-dimensional topographical projection of the area surrounding the H.O.P.E. facility sprang up from the centre of the table, replacing the image of the train. 'As you can see, there is only one railway line leading into the base of the mountain. That has to be the route it will follow.'

A bright red line snaked away from the base of the mountain that concealed H.O.P.E.'s headquarters and back towards France.

'Why a train?' Shelby asked. 'Surely transport by air would be safer.'

'Perhaps, but it would also be more vulnerable to airborne interception. Transport by land is also more discreet and easier to defend. I think it is safe to assume that the train's defences will be formidable – the cargo is too precious to jeopardise.'

'So we have to hit it in transit,' Wing said. 'A demanding task.'

'Indeed,' Raven replied. 'There is no margin for error.'

'There,' Otto said, 'that's where we get on board. That's the interception point.' Otto pinpointed the single location along the train's route where it would cross a river. 'Can we pull up schematics of that bridge?' he asked.

'Give me a moment.' Raven set to work at the command terminal, hunting for the data they needed. 'This would be a lot quicker if we still had H.I.V.E.mind,' she sighed after a minute or so.

'Well we don't,' Laura said sadly, 'and I really don't want to think about that too much if you don't mind. Let me have a go.'

The loss of H.I.V.E.mind, the sophisticated artificial intelligence that had once controlled the school's network, was still acutely felt by them all. He had sacrificed himself to save them from Number One's insane plans but the nobility of the act did nothing to lessen the loss they all felt. H.I.V.E.mind had been more than just a computer program; he had been their friend and ally.

Raven stepped aside and Laura took over at the terminal, her fingers flying over the keyboard.

'Got it,' Laura said after a few seconds and a detailed schematic of the bridge in question popped up.

'Yeah, that's good,' Shelby said, studying the bridge, 'it's doable. Good suspension points here and here.'

'Would it not be easier to simply have a Shroud drop us directly on to the train?' Wing asked.

'Too risky,' Otto said, 'that thing's bound to have anti-air-defence systems. The Shroud's stealth systems are good but we have to assume that they have countermeasures. Besides which, at the speeds we're talking about, the

slightest mistake and . . .'

'They'd be bringing us home in a bucket,' Shelby said.

'A very small bucket,' Otto said with a grim smile.

'Two teams,' Shelby continued, 'one front, one back. Both work towards the centre carriage, which is where I would assume they'll have the cargo. Double the chances of success.'

'Makes sense,' Otto replied. 'Me and Wing at one end, Laura and Shelby at the other.'

'Once we're on the outer hull our camo suits should screen us from any external sensors . . .'

'No!' Raven said quickly. 'Darkdoom's orders – no suits. If this goes wrong we don't want H.O.P.E. getting their hands on any more thermoptic camo, we do this the old-fashioned way.'

'Jeez,' Shelby sighed, 'he didn't think this would be hard enough as it is?'

'You will respect the orders of your superiors, Miss Trinity,' Raven said, a sudden edge to her tone. 'I'm sure I do not need to remind you of the punishment for insubordination.'

Raven's reprimand caught Shelby off guard. She opened her mouth as if to say something else but thought better of it when she saw the look in Raven's eyes.

'No suits then,' Otto said quickly, 'but if I can get on to the hull I can probably disable any sensors remotely.'

'Probably?' Laura said, raising an eyebrow.

'Who knows what that thing's equipped with,' Otto replied. 'We're going to be improvising here. I should be able to blind that thing externally but only if I can get close enough.'

'Once we're on board, then what?' Laura asked.

'Two priorities,' Otto replied. 'First we have to secure

13

that camo suit and second we have to see if we can stop the train itself or at least slow it down.'

'I think you guys should leave the retrieval to me and Laura,' Shelby said quickly. 'I have some experience with this kind of thing.' They all knew what Shelby was referring to; she had after all been one of the world's most notorious and successful cat burglars before she had been inducted into H.I.V.E. The world's security forces were still searching for the Wraith, as Shelby had been known in her previous life. They had no idea that they had in fact been looking for a teenage girl.

'This isn't a piece of priceless jewellery or an artefact in a museum,' Otto replied. 'That train is going to be filled with automated defence systems. I think it would be best if we left that side of the operation to me and Wing. You guys just concentrate on stopping the thing, safer for everyone that way.'

'Since when is any of this safe?' Shelby said indignantly. 'There's nothing that you and Wing can handle that we can't take care of just as easily.'

'Otto is right,' Wing said calmly. 'It would be better if you left the retrieval side of the operation to us. Otto's abilities will allow us to access the train more quickly and easily. There is no need to expose yourselves to extra unnecessary risk.'

'Unnecessary risk? Who died and made you my guardian angel?' Shelby said angrily. 'How about you guys stopping the train and me and Laura making sure that the snatch gets done right.'

'Sounds good to me,' Laura said crossly. 'Like Shelby said, there's nothing that you can do that we can't.'

'Oh really?' Otto shot back. 'Didn't seem that way in the grappler cavern earlier –'

'You might not be able to cheat your way out of this one, binary brain,' Shelby snarled.

'That is enough!' Raven snapped. 'The success of this mission depends on you working as a team. This is no time for petty rivalries. You are all capable of successfully completing this mission or we wouldn't be sitting here now. The retrieval of the suit is our primary objective here and two teams will double our chances of success.'

She looked slowly around the table. Both Otto and Shelby looked like they had more to say but the scowl on Raven's face made them decide against it.

'The plan is sound, as far as it goes,' Raven continued. 'Both teams will work towards securing the cargo and only then attempt to stop the train to facilitate your escape. I don't want to hear any more childish squabbling.'

Raven stood up and pushed her chair back under the table. 'I'm going to prep the Shroud for launch. You should head to the Science and Technology department, Professor Pike has some special equipment for you that will help with this task. We're wheels-up in thirty minutes, so get moving.'

She watched as the four students filed out of the room in silence. Not for the first time that day she found herself wondering if she was right to send them on a mission like this. There were times when those disputes had to be put aside and individuals had to come together and function as a cohesive unit. She hoped that Otto, Shelby and the others understood that. Their lives might very well depend on it.

☣ ☣ ☣

'Now, place the power core into the housing very carefully,' Professor Pike said, positioning the glowing blue orb

that he was holding into the brushed steel casing on the workbench. 'There is always the potential for an unexpected discharge with a device like this and that would be . . . unpleasant.'

The steel casing lit up with an array of dancing blue lights as the power core brought it to life with a low hum.

'Go ahead,' the Professor said and the Alpha students sitting at the workbenches around the room proceeded to copy his actions, gingerly placing their own glowing power cores into the casings in front of them.

'This is being easy,' Franz Argentblum said with a smile as he cautiously lowered the metal ball into the machine.

'Just be careful,' Nigel Darkdoom said nervously as he watched his friend work. 'I'm still not sure that we got the distribution couplings aligned right.'

'You are worrying too much,' Franz said with a snort, 'this is like taking sweets from the baby.'

The power core locked into place with a click and the device on the workbench lit up with a hum.

'See, there is being nothing to it,' Franz said happily.

Suddenly the low hum began to rise in pitch and the lights on the exterior began to pulse more quickly and erratically.

'Is it supposed to do that?' Franz asked, swallowing nervously.

'I don't think so,' Nigel said, slowly backing away from the workbench.

'Erm . . . Professor Pike,' Franz shouted, 'I am thinking that we are having the problem.'

Professor Pike glanced up from the workbench nearby where he had been assessing another pair of students' work. He looked at the machine, now pulsing with an angry red light on Nigel and Franz's bench, just as it began

to emit an unearthly screeching noise.

'Good God!' the Professor shouted. 'Everybody get down NOW!'

The students all around the room dived for cover under the heavy metal tables as bright white, arcing bolts of electricity started to shoot from the screaming device, leaving smoking black scars on the surfaces they struck. Nigel had never seen Franz move so fast as the pair of them sprinted away from their workbench and dived behind another table. There was a final high-pitched scream discharged from the device and it exploded in a shower of sparks, half-molten lumps of metal flying in all directions. After a moment of dead silence people all around started coughing as thick, dark grey smoke filled the room.

'Is anybody hurt?' the Professor asked, slowly climbing back to his feet. Fortunately, everybody seemed to be unharmed, which was more than could be said for the area surrounding Nigel and Franz's workbench. The table was still there but where the power core and its casing had once been there was now just a large hole, its edges glowing white hot. The walls all around the table were criss-crossed by deep black scars.

'Mr Darkdoom, Mr Argentblum, would you care to explain what just happened?' the Professor said with a sigh, surveying the wreckage.

'Erm . . . equipment malfunction?' Nigel said sheepishly.

The table that they had been working on finally gave in to the damage it had sustained, collapsing with a crash.

'Yes, the faulty equipment,' Franz said hopefully. 'That is being the only explanation.'

Suddenly the door to the classroom hissed open and Otto, Wing, Laura and Shelby walked cautiously into the room.

'Did we come at a bad time?' Shelby asked, looking round at the chaos.

'Looks like an ordinary day in the Science and Technology department to me,' Otto said quietly to Wing.

'Indeed,' Wing replied, 'though there appear to be fewer fatalities than one might normally expect.'

'Ah, yes, good, you're here,' the Professor said. 'Doctor Nero had informed me that you were on your way. Come with me please.' The Professor gestured for the four new arrivals to follow him as he headed towards a door at the back of the room.

'You guys OK?' Laura asked Nigel and Franz.

'Just about,' Nigel replied. 'Though I think we may have failed the practical part of the test.'

'Shame the Explosives and Demolitions test was last week,' Otto said with a grin. 'You guys would have aced it with this.'

'I am thinking we should pass the test,' Franz said hopefully. 'Our device was working extremely well, just for a shorter time than anticipated.'

Nigel sighed and shook his head as the others filed past and followed Professor Pike through the door.

'What is going on with them?' Franz asked as he watched them leave.

'I don't know,' Nigel replied, 'but let's face it, with those four no one ever knows.'

☻☻☻

Raven walked around the outside of the brand new second generation Shroud dropship completing her final preflight checks, tapping quickly on the touch-sensitive screen of her hand-held tablet. Nero walked across the hangar bay towards her, noting with satisfaction that the repairs to

the area appeared to be finally nearing completion.

'Ready to go?' he asked.

'Almost,' she replied, 'just finishing refuelling.'

'Good,' Nero said. 'Are Malpense and the others ready?'

'Professor Pike is briefing them on their equipment now,' Raven replied. 'I can't really say that I like dropping them into a situation like this.'

'I wish there was another way,' Nero said with a sigh.

'I just wish we had some pilots,' Raven said, gesturing towards the Shroud. 'I know we weren't expecting to recommence airborne operations until next month but if we had someone else who could fly this mission then at least I could join them on board the train.'

'We're improvising here, Natalya,' Nero said quietly. 'We have to make do with what we've got. You're the only one who's qualified to fly a close-support mission like this.'

'I understand,' Raven said, 'and I know how capable the four of them are but they're still young and inexperienced, despite everything they've been through. I don't like sending them in without more support.'

'I share your concerns,' Nero said, 'but need I remind you how old you were when we first met?'

'I suppose you're right,' Raven said with a slight smile.

'We're training our students to be the most deadly and feared operatives on the planet,' Nero said. 'If we don't give them the chance to demonstrate what they are capable of, how can we expect them to be ready for what the future holds. You know as well as I do what the world outside these walls is like for G.L.O.V.E. agents. They will undoubtedly face much worse than this in the years to come.'

'I understand that,' Raven replied with a frown, 'but this feels like a trap, you have to sense that too.'

'Of course I do, but this technology is too valuable – we have to stop that train and its cargo from reaching its destination. H.O.P.E.'s scientists must not be allowed to reverse-engineer it. If this is a trap then we shall have to spring it and hope that luck is on our side.'

'You know I don't believe in luck,' Raven replied quietly.

'Nobody survives in this game for as long as we have without a little good fortune, Natalya, surely you've learnt that over all these years.'

'I've only learnt one thing,' Raven replied with a grim smile, 'luck is like time. It always runs out.'

chapter three

Professor Pike led Otto and the others through the door at the back of the Science and Technology department and into his personal workshop area.

'I'm afraid that I've not had as much time as I would like to prepare the equipment you will need for this mission,' he said, gesturing for them to follow him over to a brightly lit workbench in the centre of the cluttered room. 'But hopefully you should find at least some of this useful.'

First he picked up what looked like a slightly bulkier version of the standard wrist-mounted grappler unit that they were all familiar with.

'This is something that I've been working on for a while. It functions just like a standard grappler unit but as you can see there is a secondary unit here. That is a directed electromagnetic pulse gun, useful for disabling surveillance devices and security systems. The number of shots you can fire is limited but it should still prove adequate for your circumstances. Any questions?' the Professor asked.

'Will they be in the shops for Christmas?' Otto asked with a grin.

'Please try to take this seriously, Mr Malpense,' the Professor said with a sigh. 'These are not toys.'

He placed the modified grappler on the workbench and moved over to a dummy standing against the far wall that was wearing black, sculpted body armour and a helmet.

'As you have no doubt been informed, the use of therm-optic camouflage has been forbidden on this mission. This is a standard-issue armoured infiltration suit but I've recently made a couple of modifications that you should find useful. The gloves and boots are coated with a flexible electromagnetic sheath, which, once activated, should enable you to attach yourself to any metallic surface. The battery in the suit is powerful, but this function uses a lot of charge so use it sparingly. If the battery dies you will lose adhesion, which might be . . . unfortunate.'

'One of these would have made my old job much easier,' Shelby said with a grin.

'This switch triggers a full discharge of the battery through the outer skin. It should stun any person in contact with the suit but it will also leave you with no power for the rest of the systems. Very much a one-shot deal, I'm afraid.'

The Professor lifted one of the helmets from the dummy. 'Standard tactical helmet, night vision, thermal optics, the usual.'

The Professor turned back towards the armoured suit and lightly tapped a disc-shaped object attached to the breastplate of the armour.

'And finally, here we have a high-explosive limpet mine that can be detached from the suit and attached to almost any surface. You've all had explosives-handling training so I'm sure you don't need me to remind you to be careful when setting the timer. The blast radius is quite considerable.'

'Does anyone else think that walking around with a bomb on your chest might not be a very good idea?' Laura asked.

'Oh, the device is quite inert until activated, Miss

Brand,' the Professor replied, his tone matter of fact. 'The chances of accidental detonation are really quite small.'

'How reassuring,' Wing said under his breath.

'I think that covers everything,' the Professor said. 'Your equipment has already been loaded aboard the Shroud. I suggest you take advantage of the time it takes to fly to your target by familiarising yourselves more fully with the operation of your infiltration suits.'

The Professor's Blackbox communicator chirped into life and he quickly answered it. The screen lit up with the face of Dr Nero.

'The Shroud is standing by for take-off. Have you finished briefing the students?' Nero asked.

'Yes, Doctor Nero, they are on their way,' the Professor replied as Otto and the others hurried out of the room, heading for the hangar bay.

'Anyone else think that we could do with a little more time to prep for this?' Laura asked, looking worried.

'Hey, that's life at H.I.V.E.,' Otto said with a smile, 'ten per cent planning, ninety per cent wild improvisation.'

'Just once it'd be nice if we weren't making it up as we went along, though,' Shelby said, 'you know?'

'There are occasions when it is best that one is not given too much time to think about what one has to do,' Wing replied. 'I suspect that this is one such situation.'

'Besides, Shel, you've got nothing to worry about with me and Wing looking after you,' Otto said with a grin.

'You looking after us?' Shelby shot back. 'That'll be the day. I seem to remember that it's usually me and Laura who end up nurse-maiding you two.'

'Are you two planning on doing this all the way to the target?' Laura asked with a sigh. 'Because if you are, it's going to be a really long flight.'

'OK, OK,' Shelby said with a smile, 'let's settle this once and for all. If me and Laura get to the suit first, you guys have to do all of our Political Corruption assignments for the next three months.'

Otto whistled. 'Those are very high stakes. And when me and Wing beat you to the target, what then?' he said confidently.

'Never gonna happen,' Shelby replied, 'but just for the sake of argument, if you do we'll do all of your assignments. Deal?'

'Deal,' Otto said. 'Hope you like writing essays.'

'Pfft, dream on, chips for brains,' Shelby said.

'I'm not sure that this is such a good idea,' Wing said to Laura as Otto and Shelby continued winding each other up.

'What's the matter?' Laura asked with a grin. 'Scared?'

'Of three months of Political Corruption assignments?' Wing said. 'Of course. Who in their right mind would not be?'

☻☻☻

Raven watched from the cockpit window as Otto, Wing, Laura and Shelby crossed the hangar bay towards the Shroud. She fired up the engines on the powerful aircraft; all of the readouts were in the green.

At the bottom of the loading ramp Nero stood waiting as the four students approached.

'Are you all ready for this?' Nero said over the roar of the Shroud's engines.

'Ready as we can be,' Otto replied. 'Anything else we should know before we get airborne?'

'Nothing that would help,' Nero replied. 'Just make sure that you either retrieve or destroy that suit. It would

24

be nice to get at least a couple of you back relatively intact too.'

'We'll see what we can do,' Otto replied with a crooked smile.

Nero stood aside to let them board the loading ramp, which whirred shut behind them, and he retreated to a safe distance as the roar of the engines became louder.

Inside the Shroud Otto and the others strapped themselves into their seats, ready for take-off.

'Everybody on board?' Raven's voice crackled over the cabin intercom.

'Seatbacks and tables in the upright and locked position,' Shelby said as the muffled sound of the engines increased in pitch.

'Roger that,' Raven replied. 'Let's get this show on the road.'

Nero watched as the Shroud lifted slowly off the pad, the huge crater doors overhead grinding aside, flooding the concealed hangar with daylight. The Shroud's nose tilted upwards and with a deafening roar it rose out of the crater into the clear blue sky.

☣ ☣ ☣

Sebastian Trent watched as the H.O.P.E. technicians made the final preparations for the departure of the train that would carry the captured thermoptic camouflage suit to their headquarters in the Alps. He was not a patient man and the hours it had taken to prepare the armoured carriages for departure had done nothing to improve his mood. A worried looking technician approached.

'Report,' Trent snapped.

'We should be ready for departure in less than an hour,' the technician replied anxiously. 'We had to iron

out a couple of final glitches in the systems but we're very nearly there.'

'Good,' Trent replied with a thin smile. 'I will hold you personally responsible should any last-minute technical problems arise.'

'All countermeasures are functioning as expected, sir,' the man replied. 'We are confident of success.'

Trent dismissed the man with a cursory wave of his hand. He could not afford for there to be any unexpected problems now. After the humiliating defeat he had suffered at the hands of G.L.O.V.E. just a few months previously, he had barely managed to keep the details secret from his peers in the world's security services. What he had not been able to conceal was the fact that Maximilian Nero had slipped through his fingers. It had been a huge blow to both H.O.P.E.'s and his own credibility; questions had been asked at the highest levels about his suitability to continue as H.O.P.E.'s commander. If they had known what had really happened and the extent to which he had been secretly involved with Number One's unsuccessful plot for world domination, they would not just have been thinking about replacing him, they would have locked him up and thrown away the key. He had been forced to carry out a ruthless purge of his own staff to ensure that no one would ever reveal the truth. Another disaster like that and he doubted very much that either he or H.O.P.E. would survive. There was a lot riding on this operation – if he was successful today he knew he would no longer have to worry about any of these things.

H.O.P.E.'s head of security approached, looking concerned.

'Sir, we've loaded the cargo on board. Are you sure you won't reconsider and allow some of my men to travel with

it?' the uniformed officer asked.

'And how could you ensure that none of your men are agents working for our enemies?' Trent sneered. 'We have seen G.L.O.V.E.'s ability to infiltrate men into some of the most trusted positions in the security services time and time again. I do not trust people but I do trust machines.' He gestured to the armoured carriages outside. 'The only way to be certain of transporting a cargo this sensitive is to remove the human factor from the equation altogether.'

'But, sir . . .'

'Do not question my orders again,' Trent shouted angrily, 'or I shall see to it personally that you are posted to our Alaskan facility for the rest of your natural life. You are dismissed.'

The head of security retreated out of the room without another word. Trent looked down at the train again, a smile twitching at the corner of his mouth.

'Your move, Nero . . . your move.'

chapter four

Otto sat on board the Shroud with his eyes closed, listening to the gentle rumble of the engines. Raven had engaged the stealth field shortly after take-off and the Shroud was now, to all intents and purposes, invisible. Its outer hull employed similar technology to a thermoptic camouflage suit, projecting a holographic field around the aircraft that made it disappear from view. That, coupled with its non-existent radar signature, meant that even the most sophisticated aircraft-tracking systems would be unable to detect it, much less intercept it. None of that changed the fact that nearly every time Otto had been on board one of the things he had found himself flying into life-threatening situations.

He ran over the plan for the interception of the train in his mind again. The more he turned the problems and alternative scenarios over in his head, the more he realised that there were just too many unknown quantities. He was sure that were it not for his own unique abilities he would never have been selected for this mission and neither his friends' or his own life would have been put at risk like this. Not for the first time in the past few months he found himself wondering if the skills that had been engineered into him at birth were more of a curse than a blessing.

'Please don't tell me you're asleep,' Laura said, flopping down in the seat next to him.

'You're joking, aren't you?' Otto replied, opening his eyes. 'I'm not sure even a Sleeper blast would put me out at this point.'

'I know what you mean,' Laura replied quietly, 'never mind the amount of adrenaline pumping round my system. I'm sure that they deliberately made it impossible to find a comfortable sitting position in this body armour.'

'Wing would tell you that "discomfort brings focus", you know,' Otto said, grinning.

'If focus is the same thing as a numb backside then he might just be right,' Laura laughed and then fell silent.

'You OK?' Otto said, looking at Laura.

'Aye, just nervous,' she replied with a slight smile. 'I suppose I should be used to this sort of thing by now.'

'I don't think you ever get used to it,' Otto said quietly. 'I think you just have to learn to deal with it. We'll be OK.'

'I know, it just helps to talk about it, especially to you . . .'

Laura was interrupted by Shelby storming back to her seat from the front of the compartment.

'Damn it!' she shouted. 'How are we supposed to move in these things? I might as well be wearing plate mail.' She squirmed inside her body armour, trying in vain to get it to sit comfortably on her shoulders.

'I don't think they were designed for comfort,' Otto replied.

'Yeah, I think that stopping a bullet may have been a slightly higher priority,' Laura replied with a chuckle.

'Besides, it doesn't seem to be bothering everyone,' Otto said, gesturing towards the rear of the compartment, where Wing sat, fast asleep and snoring gently.

'How does he do that?' Shelby said in amazement.

'I wish I knew,' Otto said with a grin, 'I really do.'

⊛⊛⊛

Trent watched as the train pulled away from the platform, slowly picking up speed.

'All systems engaged, bio-digital interface running at full capacity,' reported a technician monitoring a screen nearby.

'Very good,' Trent replied, and turning to the head of security said, 'inform the facility in the Alps that the package is on its way.'

'Yes, sir,' the man replied and picked up the communications handset next to his workstation.

Trent walked out of the control centre and out on to the balcony overlooking the track, watching as the end of the train slowly disappeared around a bend. A smile slowly spread across his face; he had waited a long time for this. By the end of the day arguably the most valuable technology on the planet would be in the hands of H.O.P.E.'s scientists and the first step towards the final destruction of G.L.O.V.E. would have been taken. Nothing could stop that now.

⊛⊛⊛

Raven activated the Shroud's autopilot and climbed down the short ladder to the compartment below. She found Otto, Shelby and Laura checking each other's body armour, chatting quietly. She couldn't help but smile as she saw Wing sitting upright, fast asleep at the rear of the compartment. She walked over to him and gently shook his shoulder. Wing's eyes flicked open; there was none of the disorientation in his face that one would normally expect when someone had just woken up, just a calm

30

determination. She gestured for him to follow her to where the others were standing.

'So have you familiarised yourself with your body armour?' Raven asked.

'Yeah, it's great other than the fact that I feel like I'm wearing a deep-sea diving suit,' Shelby said, sounding irritated.

'You get used to it,' Raven replied. 'I know that the suits must seem slightly cumbersome but they offer unparalleled personal protection.'

'How far out are we?' Otto asked.

'About twenty minutes. Is there anything you need?' Raven replied.

'A detailed schematic of the interior of the target would be nice,' Wing replied, raising an eyebrow.

'I still can't give you that,' Raven replied, smiling slightly, 'but I do have something else that might come in handy.' She moved to the lockers that lined the back wall of the compartment and opened one.

'One for you,' she said, pulling a long, thin scabbard from the locker and throwing it to Wing, 'and one for you.' She threw the second sword to Shelby.

Wing smiled as he pulled the black-bladed katana from its sheath. He pressed a button on the hilt of the weapon and the cutting edge of the blade lit up with a dark purple corona of crackling energy. They had all seen Raven's weapons in action before. The energy field could be set to give a blunted non-lethal striking surface or, at the other extreme, a mono-molecular edge that could slice straight through armoured steel. The weapons never normally left the crossed scabbards on Raven's back but now she was entrusting them to Wing and Shelby.

'Careful with those,' Raven said with a twisted smile.

'They may well come in handy but I don't really want to have to explain any accidental self-inflicted amputations to Nero, if you don't mind.'

'Thanks . . . I think,' Shelby said, gingerly holding the glowing blade out in front of her.

'Now, I know that Wing is the only one of you that is trained to use these properly in combat,' Raven said, 'but, Shelby, you may well find it useful for gaining access to the interior of the target. Please do try not to lose them, Professor Pike gets extremely irritated when he has to build replacements.'

Raven quickly strapped the scabbards to Wing and Shelby's backs.

'Do you get the feeling that she's worried about this?' Laura whispered to Otto as Raven checked that Wing and Shelby could reach their new weapons easily.

'Maybe just a little,' Otto replied quietly. 'To be honest, I'm trying really hard right now not to think about the fact that we're about to drop ourselves into a situation that would make *her* nervous.'

'That makes two of us,' Laura said with an anxious smile.

Raven finished adjusting the position of the sword on Shelby's back, apparently satisfied that she could draw the weapon quickly and easily.

'OK, time to get your helmets on,' Raven said briskly. 'When I give you the green light, take up your positions by the ramp. When the ramp drops move quickly but carefully, we're only going to get one shot at this.'

Otto and the others headed quickly to the equipment racks as Raven climbed back up the ladder to the cockpit. She stopped halfway up and looked down at them.

'Call for evac if you need it,' she said calmly. 'That

suit's important but it's not worth dying for.'

The four of them watched as Raven disappeared into the cockpit.

'The suit may not be worth dying for,' Otto said to Wing quietly, 'but three extra months of Political Corruption assignments . . . that's another matter.'

☢ ☢ ☢

The H.O.P.E. control centre bustled with activity as the technicians tracked the progress of the train speeding along its predetermined course. Trent turned away from the large display on the wall and beckoned his head of security over.

'Issue the updated mission parameters,' Trent said quietly. 'I think we have waited long enough.'

'Yes, sir,' the man replied and moved quickly to a nearby terminal.

Around the room an updated mission briefing popped up on the screens of the technicians and security personnel who were monitoring the train's progress. Trent watched as his men read the updated mission briefing, noting with a certain amount of pleasure the surprised expressions on their faces.

'Can you cover me for a couple of minutes?' one of the technicians asked his neighbour. 'I need to use the bathroom.'

'OK,' the other man replied, 'but you'd better be quick, I wouldn't want to be you if Trent catches you away from your station.'

'I know, I know,' the technician replied, 'I'll be as quick as I can.'

The technician got up from his station and headed out of the control centre and along the corridor to the

restrooms. Once inside he hurried into one of the cubicles. He waited for a moment, listening carefully, and once he was satisfied that there was no one else there he reached down and took off his shoe. He removed the insole, pulled out a tiny metallic object and quickly popped it into his ear. He tapped on the tiny device and waited for a couple of seconds before a woman's voice came through the tiny transmitter.

'Check in, please,' the woman said in his ear.

'Agent 1574,' the technician whispered quickly, 'urgent comms for Darkdoom.'

'Director Darkdoom is unavailable at this time,' the woman replied, 'send message for priority relay. We will –' The woman's voice was cut off by a burst of static.

The technician cursed under his breath.

'Message is as follows,' the technician said quietly, hoping that he could still be heard at the other end, 'target's mission parameters are changed. Repeat, mission parameters are changed. Abort retrieval operation immediately. Target is not as originally reported . . .'

The door to the cubicle flew open and the technician recoiled as he saw the silencer of the automatic pistol. The gun coughed as it was fired twice, putting two rounds into the chest of the startled technician, who slumped backwards. H.O.P.E.'s head of security reached forward and plucked the tiny transmitter from the dead technician's ear and dropped it on to the tiled floor of the toilet, crushing it under his boot heel. He pulled out his own communications device and spoke into it quickly.

'The leak is plugged, Commander Trent,' he said.

'Excellent,' Trent's voice crackled over the communicator. 'Did he manage to send a warning?'

'No, sir, we jammed his comms before he could do

34

any harm.'

'Very well. He had outlived his usefulness anyway,' Trent replied. 'Have the body disposed of and then return to the control centre immediately. I want you here when our guests arrive.'

'Understood.'

☻☻☻

Raven gently nudged the joystick bringing the Shroud in slowly and carefully over the target. Through the cockpit window she could see the dark shape of the bridge looming out of the darkness ahead. She brought the dropship to a hover over the highest point of the superstructure and hit the controls to open the rear loading ramp.

Down in the cargo compartment Otto took a deep breath as the ramp lowered with a mechanical whirring sound. In the darkness outside he could just make out the huge metal girders that formed the skeletal frame of the bridge. He activated the night-vision mode of his helmet and looked to his left as Wing gave him the thumbs-up.

Otto, Laura and Shelby followed him down to the edge of the ramp. Just below them was a steel platform with a maintenance gantry leading away in both directions along the bridge. Wing hopped off the ramp and down on to the platform with the others close behind.

As Otto climbed down on to the narrow platform he felt the wind whipping around him. He could feel the chill at this altitude, even through his body armour.

'Down and clear,' Otto said.

'Roger that,' Raven replied in his ear, 'moving to stand-off position.'

Behind them the ramp closed, the window of red light that came from the cargo bay disappearing into the night

as the Shroud's stealth field was sealed again. There was a brief gust of wind as the invisible craft moved away from the bridge, leaving the four of them alone.

'Let's go,' Shelby said. After moving twenty metres or so along the gantry she stopped and climbed carefully over the safety railing, pausing for just a moment before walking out along one of the foot-wide horizontal girders that spanned the apex of the bridge. She moved quickly to the target location before removing her backpack and taking out a series of small metallic boxes which she placed at four different points along the girder's length. There was a loud popping sound as she deployed the explosive-charged bolts on each device, securing them in position.

'OK, suspension units secure,' Shelby said. 'Ready when you are.'

Wing was next over the railing, moving quickly along the girder to the position next to Shelby. Otto followed just behind, stepping gingerly down. Anyone who had watched Shelby and Wing walk along the girder would have thought that they were out for a casual afternoon stroll, but Otto found it rather harder to ignore the long drop to the deck of the bridge far below. A slip here would undoubtedly be fatal.

'Remember,' Shelby said with a chuckle as Otto moved slowly along the beam, 'it's not the fall that kills you, it's the sudden stop at the bottom.'

'Thanks for that,' Otto said, trying to ignore her. After a few more steps he reached his suspension unit and knelt down carefully. He detached the clip from the side of the box and pulled out a metre or so of the thin cable from the reel inside. He reached behind his back and attached the clip to the harness built into his armour. He let out a long relieved sigh. Now at least he was attached to

something. He looked back to the maintenance gantry as Laura slowly moved along the girder and completed the same procedure.

'All set?' Shelby asked.

'Good to go,' Otto replied.

'Ready,' Wing said, lowering himself to sit on the girder, his legs dangling in the void below them.

'This cable's awfully thin,' Laura said quietly.

'The breaking strain on this line is over three tons,' Wing replied calmly.

'So only Shelby's got anything to worry about,' Otto said quickly, making Laura laugh.

'Gee, you're a funny guy, I sure hope I secured your suspension unit correctly,' Shelby shot back.

'That's enough,' Raven said, her transmission cutting into their chatter. 'Target is sixty seconds out, get into position.'

Otto took a deep breath and lowered himself over the edge of the girder, feeling a fleeting moment of dizzying vertigo as he swung gently in mid-air.

'You know, this seemed like a good idea a few hours ago,' Laura said quietly, fighting to keep the edge of panic from her voice.

Otto tried to stay calm as they all hung there, a few feet below the girder, for what seemed like an eternity, and then the bridge began to vibrate very slightly as their target raced towards them. Otto looked down and saw the lights from the front of the train illuminating the track far below.

'Go!' Shelby said and they all simultaneously triggered the releases on the cable brakes. For a moment Otto felt the sickening feeling of free fall in his stomach as he plummeted towards the tracks. Time seemed to slow down

as they fell and for the briefest moment Otto wondered if they'd gone too early, but then the top of the train carriages shot past below him. The release on the clip in the small of his back triggered automatically and he fell the last couple of feet on to the roof of the train just as the magnetic surface of his gloves and boots activated. He lay spreadeagled a few metres from Wing, now firmly attached to the roof of the train as it rocketed over the bridge and into the tunnel on the other side of the gorge. He tried to lift his head slightly to see if Shelby and Laura had landed at the front of the train as planned but it was impossible to see that far ahead.

'Check in,' Otto said, praying that everything had gone according to plan.

'We're on board,' Shelby's voice replied in his ear.

'Aye,' Laura said quickly. 'Is it too late to change my mind about this?'

'Any sign of an access point near you?' Wing asked.

'Negative,' Shelby replied, 'nothing obvious. Will report back when we've cleared the tunnel.'

Otto tried to ignore the battery-level indicator on his head-up display that was slowly ticking downwards. The wind tore at his body as the train raced along – if the electromagnets in his suit ran out of power he knew that he'd be thrown from the roof instantly. They had a couple of minutes, at best, to find a way inside.

chapter five

Raven brought the Shroud sweeping around the rocky flanks of the mountain. Through the cockpit window she could now see the point at which the train would exit the tunnel and she found herself holding her breath as she waited for the hurtling carriages to emerge. She knew that there was no way she could check in with them until then and the feeling of powerlessness was deeply frustrating. Suddenly the train shot out of the tunnel. She switched the cockpit's head-up display to thermal mode and breathed a long sigh of relief as she counted the four distinct heat signatures on the roof. She quickly thumbed her communicator.

'Raven to infiltration team,' she said quickly, 'sit rep.'

'All down and in one piece,' Otto's voice came back, 'moving to secure access points now.'

'Roger that,' Raven replied. She thumbed another button on the communicator's control panel and spoke again. 'Raven to control, they're on board.'

'Understood,' Nero's voice replied, 'keep me updated.'

☺ ☺ ☺

'External sensors indicate that we've picked up some passengers,' one of the H.O.P.E. technicians reported, 'should we deploy countermeasures?'

'No,' Trent said calmly, studying the readouts of the train's telemetry. 'Wait till they get inside, stick to the plan.'

'Yes, sir,' the technician replied.

'Once we have confirmed the identities of our uninvited guests we can move to neutralise them,' Trent said, smiling.

So far, everything was going exactly as he had planned.

☹ ☹ ☹

'Still got no obvious access points here,' Shelby reported as the train thundered along in the darkness. 'Do your stuff, Otto.'

Otto closed his eyes, trying to ignore the wind whistling past him as he reached out with his mind to connect with the computers that controlled the train. Something was wrong; he could sense the simple computers controlling his and Wing's suit systems but there was nothing coming from the train at all. It appeared as nothing more than a deep, black void in the digital space his mind drifted through.

'There's nothing there,' Otto said quietly, feeling a twinge of panic. 'The systems must be shielded somehow.'

'Nothing?' Laura replied. 'That's not good, we've got no obvious access points here. We need you to find us a way inside.'

'I'm trying,' Otto said, 'but there's nothing, nothing at all. It's got to be some kind of external shielding. We'll have to find another way to get inside.'

'No time for subtle then,' Shelby replied. 'Wing, can these pig stickers that Raven gave us cut through the roof?'

'Only one way to find out,' Wing replied. He forced himself slowly to his knees, fighting against the roaring winds that threatened to pluck him off the train at any moment. Reaching over his shoulder, he pulled the

katana from its scabbard, activating the energy field that surrounded the blade and switching it to the monomolecular setting. Wielding the blade in one hand, he drove it down into the roof of the carriage, sending a shower of sparks whirling into the slipstream around the train. He pulled the hilt of the blade across the roof, sending more sparks flying as he carved a hole in the train's metallic skin.

'Looks like it's working, Shelby,' Otto quickly. 'You're going to have to cut your way in to

'On it,' Shelby replied. Otto looked up an her cloud of sparks fly from the front of the train. Shelby set about creating an improvised entry point for her and Laura.

Otto noticed the battery indicator on his visor display turn from green to amber.

'Make it quick, guys,' Otto said, 'our suit batteries aren't going to last much longer.'

Wing spent what seemed like minutes but could actually only have been a few seconds finishing slicing through the roof. With a crash, a metre-square section fell inwards and light poured out of the hole.

'Go!' Wing barked, sliding the sword back into its scabbard and frantically gesturing for Otto to drop down through the hole. Otto crawled forward and clumsily scrambled down through the opening, closely followed by Wing.

'Laura, Shelby, you inside too?' Otto asked, as he climbed to his feet, scanning round his new surroundings.

There was no reply, just static. He looked around again. They were in a long, dimly lit corridor that ended in a heavy steel door. The walls that surrounded them were covered in hard, white plastic panels. riage's

interior appeared to be as featureless as its exterior.

'Comms check,' Otto said quickly, but there was no reply from anyone. Otto looked at Wing and tapped the side of his helmet. Wing just shook his head. Otto pressed a button on the side of his helmet and his visor slid open with a hiss.

'You got anything?' he asked Wing as he too retracted the visor on his helmet.

'No, nothing. I suspect that something in here is jamming our comms signals,' Wing replied. 'Can you connect to any of the train's systems yet?'

Otto closed his eyes and sought desperately to reach out and interface with any of the local systems. With a mounting sense of unease he realised that there was nothing there, even now that they were inside.

'That's impossible,' Otto muttered to himself. It was inconceivable that there were no computer systems on board a train like this and yet he could detect absolutely nothing from the digital network that he had been sure would be controlling the train.

'There's still nothing there,' Otto said, opening his eyes. 'It's like everything that I might be able to connect to has been deliberately shielded somehow. But why would someone do that? It doesn't make any sense.'

'Unless they were expecting you,' Wing said, frowning.

Otto felt a chill run down his spine.

'Let's get moving,' he said, looking at the bare, white walls that surrounded them. 'The sooner we can get out of here, the better.'

☉ ☉ ☉

Laura dropped through the hole in the roof and landed with a thump on the floor. Shelby was already at the far

end of the carriage examining the door that led back down the train. Laura clambered to her feet and ran down the carriage to where her friend was standing.

'I can't raise Otto or Wing on comms,' Shelby said as she ran a hand over the featureless metal of the door.

Laura reached into her backpack and pulled out a tiny black palmtop computer. She opened it up and began to quickly enter a series of commands. She studied the display for a few moments with a slight frown.

'What's up?' Shelby asked.

'It's weird,' Laura replied, 'I'm not picking up any electromagnetic signatures. That would explain why Otto wasn't able to connect to any of the train's systems – there's no data network that I can detect anywhere on board.'

'So what are you trying to say?' Shelby asked, looking confused. 'This thing runs on clockwork?'

'Like I said, it's weird,' Laura replied.

'Well, the first question is how do we get this door open?' Shelby said. 'No control panel, no locking mechanism that I can recognise, it's just a slab of metal.'

'Cut it?' Laura asked, gesturing to Raven's katana.

'I guess,' Shelby replied, but without any warning the door hissed open, making both of the girls jump. Shelby instinctively drew the sword from her back but there was nothing on the other side of the door but another featureless white corridor.

'How did you do that?' Laura asked.

'Funny, I was about to ask you the same question,' Shelby said quietly as she stepped carefully through the doorway.

'I don't like this,' Laura said as she followed Shelby into the next carriage.

'I know what you mean,' Shelby said, scanning the

corridor for any sign of an intruder alarm system. The door behind them hissed shut again just as suddenly as it had opened.

'Guess we're going this way then,' Shelby said, advancing cautiously down the corridor.

'Looks that way,' Laura said, fighting a growing unease.

As they approached the door at the far end of the corridor Laura put a hand on Shelby's shoulder.

'Wait a second,' she said, reaching out to touch the white panels that lined the walls. 'Can you cut one of these panels out?'

Shelby nodded and slid the tip of Raven's sword into the wall. Slowly and carefully she cut downwards a few centimetres. A jet of black liquid spurted out from the incision in the wall, splattering Shelby's arm as she recoiled backwards. The viscous black goo kept spraying out of the wall for a couple of seconds and then slowed to a trickle, running down the wall and pooling on the floor of the carriage.

'What the hell . . .' Shelby said, holding her hand up as the black liquid on her glove started to crust over almost immediately. The carriage was filled with the smell of sour milk.

'Don't get any on your skin,' Laura said quickly, pulling a thin probe from the side of her palmtop.

'I wasn't planning to,' Shelby said, her nose wrinkling at the foul smell.

Laura put the tip of the probe into the pool of liquid on the floor and studied the computer's glowing screen.

'Weird,' Laura said quietly. 'Whatever this stuff is it's organic but it's not like . . .' She stopped short.

'What?' Shelby asked, noting her friend's startled expression.

'I know why Otto can't sense anything from this train,' Laura whispered. 'We have to get out of here, now!'

☢ ☢ ☢

Otto wasn't quite so surprised when the second door that they came to hissed open in front of them. What he really didn't like was the fact that it seemed as if they were being herded towards the middle of the train.

He stepped through the door with Wing right behind him and tried to make sense of what he saw. In the centre of the carriage was a circular black column surrounded at the top by a network of black tubes that led away from it and into the walls. It looked like some sort of distribution node but still he could sense no electronic emissions of any kind from it.

'What on earth is that?' Wing asked quietly.

'Your guess is as good as mine,' Otto replied, walking towards the dark column.

As he drew closer Otto could make out vague swirling patterns in the material inside the tube.

'It's liquid,' Otto said, examining the column more carefully.

'Fuel perhaps?' Wing asked. 'Some kind of hydraulic system?'

'Could be,' Otto replied, pressing his hand against the glass. It was warm.

'We should keep moving,' Wing said, frowning. 'Nothing about this is right. We should retrieve the suit and go, we do not have long before the train will reach its destination.'

'Yeah, right,' Otto said, sounding distracted. There was something at the edge of his awareness, like a whisper of data being transmitted, but it was impossible to pin down.

45

It was like no other network that he had interfaced with before. 'Let's go.'

⊛⊛⊛

'Well, look what we found,' Shelby said with a grin as they walked into the next carriage. Standing in the centre of the room was a metallic frame with the thermoptic camouflage suit suspended in it.

'Stuff the suit,' Laura said quickly, 'we've got to find Otto and Wing and get out of here.'

'Look, I know you're worried,' Shelby replied, 'but this is what we came for. I'm not leaving without it. Even if you did find a synthetic something or other in the walls.'

'A synthetic protein matrix,' Laura snapped. 'Don't you get it?'

'No, actually, I don't,' Shelby replied, examining the frame that the suit was mounted in.

'It's alive,' Laura said, sounding exasperated. 'This whole train, it's an organic computer.'

'What are you talking about?' Shelby said, carefully feeling around the edges of the frame.

Suddenly the door at the other end of the carriage hissed open and Otto and Wing appeared.

'Oh thank god, you're all right,' Laura said as she saw the pair of them.

'Look what we found,' Shelby said triumphantly, tapping the frame that surrounded the camo suit.

'Yeah, OK, you win,' Otto said, looking worried. 'Let's grab the suit and get out of here. There's something weird about this place.'

'You're right about that,' Laura said quickly. 'Did you see any of that black liquid on the way here?'

'Yeah, there's a whole tank of it back there,' Otto said,

gesturing back at the carriage they'd just come from. 'It was weird, it was almost like I could sense data being transmitted within it but it wasn't like anything I'd felt before.'

'I think I can explain,' Laura said.

'No, Miss Brand,' the unmistakeable voice of Sebastian Trent came from all around them, 'allow me.'

'Trent.' Otto spat out the name.

'It's so good to see you again, Mr Malpense,' Trent replied. 'In fact all of this would have been rather pointless if you hadn't been here.'

'What do you mean?' Otto asked.

'Oh, come now, Mr Malpense,' Trent said, sounding pleased, 'an automated train, its only apparent vulnerability its computer systems, a stealth suit that has to be retrieved. I went to a lot of trouble to make sure that Nero and Darkdoom would send you.'

'But there aren't any computer systems on this train,' Otto sneered. 'I suppose that was the idea, wasn't it?'

'Whoever said there were no computer systems?' Trent asked. 'This train is the temporary home to perhaps the most sophisticated computer system ever devised. It's all around you, Mr Malpense – the world's first living machine, a fully functional organic supercomputer that is quite immune to your powers of control. It was developed in our Paris laboratories and is being transported to our headquarters for installation. You see this is just a prototype, the first of a new generation, but once it is coupled with your unique brain and all of your special abilities it will herald a new technological dawn, a new breed of intelligent machine over which I will have unquestioned control.'

'Why would I ever help you?' Otto said angrily.

'I'm afraid that you won't have much say in the matter,' Trent replied. 'You see this machine may be immune to you, but the reverse, unfortunately for you, is not true.'

A slow, pulsing thud was coming from the walls of the train that surrounded them. It sounded like a giant's heartbeat. The sound began to rise in intensity, getting louder and louder. Suddenly Otto let out a scream of pain, falling to his knees, both hands pressed to his skull. Wing ran to Otto's side.

'Otto, what's wrong?' Wing yelled over the sound pulsating all around them.

'Get out . . .' Otto gasped, 'get out of my head . . .'

A trickle of blood ran from Otto's nose.

'Much as I'm looking forward to seeing Mr Malpense again, I'm afraid that you three are now . . . surplus to requirements,' Trent said coldly. 'But don't worry, this won't hurt too much.'

All around them the white panels that covered the carriage walls began to retract. Behind them was a network of thick black tubes emitting a dark red glow in time with the pulsing noise. For a moment nothing happened but then there was a mechanical-sounding thunk and several segmented black metal spheres rolled out of the panels and into the middle of the carriage. With a chittering sound the spheres began to unfold razor-sharp serrated limbs. Moments later the spheres had transformed into machines that looked like a cross between a crab and a spider, their backs covered in thick bands of armour, with snapping mechanical mouth parts at the front. Their metal legs made a horrible skittering sound on the metal floor of the carriage as they all turned to face the startled H.I.V.E. students.

'Oh, you have got to be kidding me,' Shelby said quietly.

'Take Otto,' Wing yelled at Laura and Shelby as he hauled Otto, now barely conscious, to his feet.

'Head back the way we came,' Wing said quickly, 'get to the rear of the train.'

Wing pulled the katana from the scabbard on his back and then reached over Shelby's shoulder and pulled its twin from her back.

Laura and Shelby hooked Otto's arms over their shoulders and started to drag his limp body down the carriage.

'Get a move on!' Wing snapped, turning to face the advancing mechanical spiders, swords raised.

The first two spider-bots dashed across the floor towards Wing with startling speed and launched themselves into the air, flying at his face. The katanas moved in a blur, flashing through the air and slicing them neatly in half, sending black liquid spraying across the white walls. The twitching halves of the creatures fell to the floor. Wing slowly backed towards the rear of the carriage after Laura and Shelby as more and more of the spiders spilled through the door at the other end.

Laura and Shelby dragged Otto down the next carriage towards the huge black column which was now pulsing with the same red glow as the tubes inside the walls. At the far end of the carriage the door slid open and dozens more of the skittering black robots poured through the doorway.

'Not good,' Laura hissed as she and Shelby set Otto down next to the column, his head resting against the black glass. Shelby raised the modified grappler unit mounted on her wrist and triggered the directed electro-magnetic pulse. A bright blue bolt of lightning shot from her wrist and struck the first of the creatures that was scuttling across the floor towards them, sending it flying

backwards in a shower of sparks.

'We've got a problem here,' Shelby yelled back towards Wing.

Wing cut down another mechanical spider in mid-air and glanced quickly over his shoulder at the tide of metallic creatures approaching from the opposite end of the carriage.

'Look out!' Laura screamed as another one flew at Wing, hitting him square in the chest, sending him staggering backwards. The creature dug its serrated feet into Wing's body armour, its razor-sharp mouth parts snapping at his face. Wing tried to push the spider off him, but it was no good, it was too strong. Its snapping jaws lashed at his face, leaving a long gash down one cheek as others swarmed towards him. One latched on to his leg, making him gasp in pain.

'Full discharge,' Wing grunted as he dropped to one knee under the weight of the robotic creatures attacking him. There was a brief high-pitched whine like a camera flash charging and then Wing's entire suit of body armour was covered in a bright white coruscating field of electrical energy. The spiders attached to him were destroyed instantly, exploding in showers of sparks, as were any others within a few metres of him. Wing staggered backwards towards Shelby and Laura, swords raised again, his smouldering armour covered in flecks of the carbonised black liquid.

Shelby and Laura continued to fire electromagnetic pulses from their wrist units into the wave of mechanical monsters pouring out of the door at the opposite end of the carriage. For every one they destroyed another two appeared through the doorway, scurrying down the carriage towards them. They were totally overwhelmed.

'Battery levels critical,' a soft mechanical voice said in Laura's ear.

'We need an exit,' Laura yelled over the sounds of the battle.

'But we still haven't retrieved the suit,' Shelby shouted back desperately.

'Raven said it's not worth dying for and I agree,' shouted Laura.

'I was just thinking the same thing,' Shelby said, pulling the disc-shaped explosive charge from her chest. She punched a short detonation delay into the controls on top of the limpet mine and hurled it towards the far end of the carriage, where it disappeared into the swarming mass of mechanical killers. Shelby turned and threw herself on top of Laura as the far end of the carriage disappeared in a ball of fire.

☣☣☣

Raven watched in horror as an explosion tore through the roof and wall of a carriage near the end of the train. The rear-most carriages bucked, their connection to the rest of the train severed, their wheels bouncing off the rails and sending them tumbling over the edge of the cliff that the tracks ran alongside. The cartwheeling carriages bounced off the cliff face a couple of times before smashing into countless blazing pieces on the valley floor far below. She silently prayed that none of her team had been in them as she jerked at the Shroud's controls, sending it diving towards the stricken train racing along the tracks, its tail ablaze. They were on the final approach to the train's destination; time was running out.

☣☣☣

Shelby rolled off Laura, coughing as the smoke from the explosion was quickly sucked out of the carriage by the wind that roared through the gaping hole where the rearmost carriages had once been.

'Are you crazy?' Laura yelled. 'You could have killed us!'

'Maybe,' Shelby said with a grim smile, 'but I thought we were running out of options.'

Wing picked himself up off the floor and looked back towards the front of the train. Still more of the robotic spiders were pouring through the door. He raised his swords again as the creatures advanced remorselessly towards him.

☢ ☢ ☢

Otto struggled to stay afloat in an endless sea of black liquid. He could feel himself weakening. Somewhere at the edge of consciousness he could hear the same whisper that he had heard when he had been near the column of black liquid on the train. All the time he could feel his own personality slipping away, submerged beneath the black tide. He forced himself to stay calm, listening to the distant whispering, straining to make any sense of what he could hear. It was no good, he wasn't strong enough and slowly, inexorably he felt himself sink below the inky, black surface. He had no fight left in him, he was about to be consumed and he was powerless to resist.

'You are not alone,' a calm, measured voice said inside his head and suddenly Otto felt an unbelievable surge of strength. He could suddenly feel the network all around him, the organic, slithering hiss of its voice clear and instantly comprehensible. He rose up out of the black sea, golden tendrils of data streaming down from his glowing

body and into the dark liquid, dazzling flashes of light beginning to burst beneath its surface.

'My turn,' Otto said with a grim smile.

☻ ☻ ☻

Laura tried to fire one last pulse from the unit on her wrist but it was no good, her suit's batteries were completely drained. She glanced across at Shelby, who shook her head in answer; her power reserves were gone too. Wing stood in front of them, desperately slashing at the creatures that were still advancing. He could feel himself beginning to tire. The robotic creatures seemed to sense his weakness, massing for one last assault.

Otto gasped explosively and his eyes flew open just as the chittering metal wave of spider-bots raced forward.

'Stop!' Otto yelled and simultaneously every one of the mechanical killers froze in its tracks. The red light began to pulse even more brightly from the column behind Otto and he gritted his teeth.

'Get out of here,' Otto hissed to his friends. 'I don't know how long I can hold them.'

'What are we going to do?' Shelby said quickly, looking back over her shoulder at the smouldering hole where the rear carriage had once been. 'Jump?'

The roar of the wind through the shattered rear of the carriage suddenly intensified and the huge, black shape of the unshielded Shroud appeared behind the train.

'Go! Now!' Otto yelled. For a moment Shelby and Laura looked as though they were going to argue but they both knew that this might be their only chance. They sprinted down the carriage towards the forward boarding ramp that was lowering from the nose of the dropship.

On board the Shroud Raven was completely focused on

keeping the aircraft at the same speed as the train to keep the ramp as near to the rear of the carriage as she could. The mountain containing H.O.P.E.'s headquarters was looming into view – they were very nearly at the end of the line and Raven tried to ignore the impending danger.

'You too,' Otto yelled at Wing.

'Not on my own,' Wing said, looking Otto straight in the eye.

'I'll be right behind you,' Otto gasped as the pulsing from the black column reached a peak. Wing stood there for a moment, before cursing under his breath and sprinting down the carriage after Laura and Shelby.

Otto could feel the organic computer fighting fiercely, desperately trying to reassert its control over the train. Otto pushed back, forcing the train to accelerate, the carriage starting to shudder as the chassis exceeded its design limits. Otto could sense the organic control system reading the train's coordinates. The end of the line was racing towards them. Almost unconsciously Otto's brain calculated the velocity of the train and the distance remaining. He tried to hold firm but with each moment that passed he could feel the organic computer wrestling to override his instructions.

With a final grunt of effort Otto locked out the train's braking system and turned and sprinted towards the gaping hole at the end of the carriage. The world seemed to slow down as he raced towards the Shroud. He could see Wing waiting at the bottom of the boarding ramp, one hand outstretched. Otto dived forward, grabbing for Wing's hand and feeling his friend's fingers close around his at the exact moment that the Shroud's engines roared and the nose ramp lurched up to close. Otto and Wing tumbled down the ramp, crashing into the cargo bay,

grabbing on to anything they could find as the Shroud reared upwards, shooting vertically into the sky, just a few metres from the rocky face of the mountain.

Below them the stricken train speared into the terminal, still travelling at over two hundred miles per hour. It leapt over the buffers at the end of the track and flew into the wall of the cavern, exploding with catastrophic force. A huge ball of fire sprang from the cave mouth, debris scattering down the sides of the mountain.

☉ ☉ ☉

'No!' Sebastian Trent screamed as they watched the monitors in the control centre, powerless to stop the train's collision course. He rounded on the nearest technician, his face red with fury.

'Launch all available interceptors. Bring that aircraft down!'

'We've lost the target, sir,' the technician replied, fear in his voice. 'They appear to have re-engaged their stealth systems.'

Trent's face was a mask of impotent rage. He turned back to the monitors that showed the clouds of black smoke billowing from the rail terminal cavern.

'Prep my helicopter, tell the Alps facility that I'm on my way. Dispatch retrieval teams for the wreckage. I want a full damage report on my desk when I arrive,' Trent snarled as he turned and stormed out of the room.

chapter six

Otto, Laura, Shelby and Wing sat on the opposite side of the briefing-room table from Dr Nero as he finished reading the last paragraph of their report on the mission.

'A satisfactory, if somewhat unsubtle resolution to the situation,' Nero said with a wry smile, closing the report. 'The suit was completely destroyed, but news of this technology that H.O.P.E. has developed is troubling. It was clearly designed with the express intention of defeating your special abilities, Mister Malpense.'

'It certainly seems that way,' Otto replied. 'What's even more worrying is that Trent said that it was just a prototype. I was barely able to exert any control over this system, I don't really want to think what the next generation of the same technology might be capable of.'

'Indeed,' Nero said, 'and I cannot think of a worse person to have control over such a system than Sebastian Trent.'

'There's something else that worries me, though,' Otto said, looking around the table. 'The system was not intelligent in the true sense of the word but it was capable of emotion.'

'What do you mean?' Nero asked with a frown.

'It's hard to explain,' Otto replied, 'but when I was inside the system I could feel it. It hates us. Not just me or any of us on the train . . . humanity . . . it hates all of us. It wasn't conscious thought, just emotion, but it was there.'

'I see,' Nero replied. 'I think that this needs further investigation.' He glanced at Raven and she nodded slightly. 'The four of you have exceeded my expectations once again. You deserve some rest. You are dismissed.'

Otto and the others rose from the table and left the briefing room.

'I need to speak to Darkdoom,' Nero said, standing up. 'If Trent had succeeded in this, if he had somehow been able to combine this new technology with Malpense's abilities . . .'

'Not a situation I would like to contemplate,' Raven replied.

'Agreed. We need to find out as much as we can about this technology and exactly what H.O.P.E. intend to do with it. Whatever they have planned, we have to be ready.'

☢ ☢ ☢

Otto sat alone at the table in the dining hall, staring into space, lost in thought.

'You should get something to eat,' Wing said as he sat down in the chair next to Otto. 'Franz was just behind me in the queue and I fear that there may be slim pickings once he has finished.'

'Aye, I've seen plagues of locusts that were less efficient,' Laura said, placing her tray on the table and sitting down on the other side of Otto.

Otto smiled weakly and then sighed.

'You all right?' Laura asked.

'Just tired,' Otto said, rubbing his temples. 'Brain-wrestling with that thing took more out of me than I'd thought.'

'What was it like?' Laura asked.

'Like drowning in an oil slick,' Otto said with a crooked smile. 'Not something I'm in any hurry to repeat. You know what was really weird though?'

'What?'

'To be perfectly honest I don't remember a lot about what happened but there was something that I can't explain. I was losing, I could feel myself slipping away but then something happened, like a sudden burst of strength. Like I say, it's hard to explain.'

'It is not unusual for people to feel sudden bursts of strength when confronted by extreme situations,' Wing said.

'Aye, like mothers lifting cars off their children, that sort of thing,' Laura said with a nod.

'I suppose,' Otto said, sounding distracted, 'but this was different somehow, it was almost like there was someone else . . .'

'Room for one more?' Shelby asked, joining them at the table.

'Always,' Wing said with a smile.

'Good, because I have a little something for you boys,' she said with a grin, reaching down into her backpack. She slid two pieces of paper across the table towards Otto and Wing.

'Hot off the presses, two Political Corruption assignments,' Shelby grinned, 'they don't have to be done till Monday, so there's no rush.'

'You're not serious,' Otto said with a chuckle.

'Miss Brand,' Shelby said, 'remind me again who it was that got to the camo suit first.'

'Why, Miss Trinity, I do believe that was us,' Laura said happily.

'You really expect us to do these?' Otto asked, shaking

his head.

'Just because you saved us all from getting eaten by robot spiders doesn't mean you can welch on a bet,' Shelby said, slapping Otto on the shoulder. 'Now you be sure to do a good job, I expect to get top marks.'

'Perhaps in future we should be more careful about who we do and do not allow to be eaten,' Wing said, raising an eyebrow.

Otto sat listening for a few moments to his friends' banter but despite the familiar chatter there was still something distracting him, something he couldn't shake, a phrase that kept rattling around inside his head.

You are not alone.

H·I·V·E

Praise for H.I.V.E.

'Exciting, clever and all in all brilliant'
Sunday Telegraph

'Full of baddies, action and lashings of humour'
Sunday Express

Richard & Judy
Best Children's
Books Winner

OTTO MALPENSE WILL RETURN . . .
MAKE SURE YOU'RE WAITING